Broken Dreams

His Warriors

Book 2

By

Ronna M. Bacon

ISBN 978-1-989000-32-8

Library and Archives Canada

Ecclesiastes 3:11   "He has made everything beautiful in its time."

Table of Contents

Prologue

She watched as the car was pulled back from the trees and the doors pried open, frustration evident. Now what, she thought? He had failed, once more he had failed. How was she to get her hands on the girl now? He had promised to bring her to her tonight. She had plans for this girl, plans to send her far away. She saw the money slipping through her hands even as the emergency personnel worked on the two.

The bodies were pulled from the car. The paramedics and police shook their head over the male driver. It was too late for him. Attention turned to the young female passenger and they worked to save her life, readying her for transport to the hospital.

Lights flashing, the ambulance sped off, taking her to the nearest hospital, an officer heading for her home. It was still touch and go, they said. She just might not make it.

The woman followed in her car, hovering near the entrance to the treatment rooms, listening to hear if the girl survived, plans changing as the night went on. She finally walked away, knowing that for now, her plans were over. At some point in the future, she would revive them. When and how, that would come.

Chapter 1

*S*taring at the line of figures in front of him, Mark Benson reached for the portfolio he had been given. Something just seemed to be wrong between the two of them; they just didn't match. He groaned when he looked at the time, his hand running through his dark brown hair. He should have been out of the office thirty minutes ago. Rising quickly, he stuffed his paperwork into his briefcase and headed for the door, waving at the receptionist as he walked quickly out. He was to meet a friend in 30 minutes for their weekly bike ride.

"Jonah? Mark. I'm on my way. Be there in 45." Mark laughed at the response he got, his teeth showing white against his tan. "I know. Numbers do get to me, don't they? Yeah, I'll tell you about it when I get there."

Mark parked, then unloaded his bike, watching for his friends. He was sure this was where they were to met, the east side of the bike trail. He reached for his helmet and fastened it as he heard his name called.

Jonah and Matthias, two of his friends, were headed his way, pushing their bikes beside them.

"About time you got here." Jonah couldn't resist teasing Mark.

"Yeah, I know. Rub it in, why don't you?" Mark searched the area. "Does something feel off to you two?"

The two men looked at one another, then back at Mark. "No. Does it to you?" Jonah spoke for the two of them.

Mark shrugged. "It does but it could just be the remnants of what I was dealing with today. I've felt someone watching me the last few days."

"I don't see how you can spend your days cooped up inside, staring at numbers. That's what it is. You need to be outside more." Jonah, a farmer, spent most of his days in the outdoors.

"Let's go. I hope we don't get any rain before we're done."

"Why? Afraid you'll melt?" Matthias laughed at the expression of Mark's face and took off before he could catch him.

An hour later, winded and sweaty, the three friends headed for the parking lot. A sudden movement to their right had them looking that way. Jonah and Matthias hit their brakes when they heard a cry from Mark and spun around to see Mark and his bike flying down a slight embankment, to end up in a crumpled tangled pile of man and bike. Dropping their bikes, they headed for him.

"911, what is your emergency?" Matthias had pulled his phone free from its holster and dialled.

"We have a bike accident on the east biking trail, about 500 yards from the parking lot." Matthias headed down to where Jonah was bending over Mark. "We're right near the large founder's statue."

Matthias stopped, bending over Mark, watching the pain etching onto his face. The two friends knew they would have to wait for the paramedics before moving the bike.

"Jonah, how is he?"

Jonah turned, a grim look on his face. "He says it's his leg. I'm worried about his back, from the angle he fell."

The two men watched as the ambulance pulled away, then turned to look around the area, puzzled at how Mark had fallen. They had given their statements to the responding officers, who were even then searching the surrounding area.

"That's not like him, Jonah. He has the best balance of all of us."

Jonah nodded. "I know. I'm heading in after him. You coming?"

Matthias nodded, his eyes still searching the area. "It's strange something would happen when he mentioned it feeling off."

Mark stared glumly at the cast on his left leg and then laid his head back to stare at the ceiling. Why, Lord? You could have got my attention some other way, couldn't you? He shifted the sling for his left arm, then leaned his head back again. He had been in the hospital for four days now and was to be released the next day, but where would he go? A broken leg and bruised and pulled ligaments in the shoulder would lay him up for a while. He sighed, knowing that he had work he needed to do that had been entrusted to him and only him. How am I to do that now, Lord?

A sound outside his door caught his attention, and he stared at the man standing looking in at him. Hazel eyes narrowed, Mark tried to place him. He should know him, he thought, but didn't. The man watched him for a few minutes, then tipped an imaginary hat and moved away, almost a smirk on his face.

Frowning, Mark sat up and tried to see where he had gone to, then laid back. He was disabled for now, he thought. I need to get back to what I was working on. There's something there I need to figure out, but I can't think of what I was puzzled over.

A knock at his door brought his head back up. His orthopaedic surgeon stood there as well as a younger woman he didn't know.

"Mark, how are you today?" The physician smiled at the grumpy look that came over Mark's face. "That good, is it? Let's check you out. If all goes as planned, you're a free man tomorrow."

Mark snorted. "Not so free." He lifted his sling and then grimaced with the pain.

The physician nodded. "You will be. Now, where are you going to be staying?"

Mark shook his head, a resigned tone in his voice when he spoke. "I have no idea. I can't get up to my apartment. There is no elevator. My family live too far away for me to go there. And my friends can't accommodate me."

"That's what I wondered. I have a solution for you." He pulled the young woman forward. "You'll be needing to get into physiotherapy as soon as we can get you there for the shoulder in the next week. The leg will take some time. Your cast will be changed to a walking cast in two weeks and if all is well, the cast will be off two weeks later. At that point, you'll be into therapy for that." He paused, not quite sure how to continue. "Julia here is a physiotherapist and runs what we used to call a convalescent home. She takes in people that need to be under care for a while until they're mobile again."

"Wait a minute! What property and where is it?"

The woman gave an unladylike snort and turned to the physician. "Just what I said, Adam. He'll fight you. I'll be back in the morning." Her eyes studied him, and he couldn't quite determine the colour. Aquamarine what the closest he could come to.

Mark watched as she turned and walked away, her blond pony tail almost reaching her waist.

Adam started to laugh. "You'll have a fight on your hand if you refuse to go." He tapped Mark's cast. "This will be why you need to go there. She has workers who will help you get around for the next few weeks. And physio will start on that shoulder next week. We need to get it mobile again."

Chapter 2

*J*ulia stood back and watched as Mark studied the front seat of her SUV, trying his best to do it on his own. She sighed and moved forward. He needed to let her help if they had any plans on getting back to her place today.

"Mr. Benson, I know you want to be independent and that will come again. Right now, you need to let me help you. If you don't, we'll still be sitting here at suppertime, and I have things I need to accomplish today." Her words were clipped and stern.

Mark glared at her. "I can do this." He tried again and slumped back into the wheelchair.

"No, not today. Now, let me help you. I assure you, I am stronger than I look." She moved into position and arm around his waist, helped him to balance and then slide onto the seat. She reached for the seat belt, then stepped back, hands in the air as he once more glared at her. Shutting the door, she pushed the chair to the back of the vehicle, and folding it, stuffed it inside, moving aside the duffel bags his friends had brought him. She stared at the briefcase as well. Did he really think he was going to be able to work? She shrugged, knowing it wasn't her problem if he did and put his progress behind.

She looked around, shivering. It wasn't a cool day by any means, a hot late summer day, but there was something she felt that made her uneasy and chilled her. *What is it, Lord? What battle am I gearing up to fight this time?* She was resigned to that. She had been fighting too many battles lately and they were wearing her out.

Sliding behind the wheel, she shot a quick glance at Mark, noting the lines of pain and fatigue.

"Do you need to stop anywhere else, or did your friends get you everything you needed?"

He looked at her, then back through the windshield. He sighed. "I need to stop at my office. There's some paperwork there I need to pick up."

"Can I do that for you instead of you having to get out?"

He shook his head. "No. I know exactly where it is. Besides, they don't know you and wouldn't let you have access to my office."

She nodded. "Give me directions, then. I'll be going in with you, so don't plan on getting in and out of the vehicle on your own."

Julia stood in the doorway of Mark's office, watching as he searched for the documents he needed. Frustration was evident.

"Can I help you in any way?"

He looked up at Julia and sighed. "Yeah. I need a folder that isn't here. It's labeled Brown Family."

She searched for him and then turned to the filing cabinet. "Can I look in there?" At his nod, she opened it, flipping through. "Here you go."

Mark stared at the folder she handed him. "I didn't put it there. How did it get in there?" He stared at the desk, his thought processes thinking through the possibilities. "Close the door, please. Is it okay if I call you Julia?" At her nod, he continued, "There is something off in here this morning. Things are moved from where I left them. This file should not have been in the cabinet. It should have been in the desk drawer." He pulled open the drawer and stared at it, a frown in place. "Julia, I don't have my phone on me. Do you have one?"

"I do." She pulled it out and handed it to him. "Why?"

"I need to take some pictures of what's in here. It's been moved around. No one should have been in this office or my desk."

"Is this related to your accident?"

Mark's eyes shot up to her. "Now that you mention it, it could be. I felt something off when I left the office that day, just couldn't put my finger on it. I thought it was because of the files I was working on. Do I have my briefcase in your car?" She nodded as he returned her phone to her, then looked around. "I need to make sure everything is locked up. There's a box behind the door there. Can you reach it for me, please?"

She watched as he sorted through the desk drawer, then pulled himself up to look through the filing cabinets. Folders were pulled and stuffed into the box.

"I think that's it for now. I'm locking my door when I leave today as well as my desk and this cabinet. There is absolutely no reason for anyone to be in here. I'm the only one who has authorized access to these files."

She nodded, then waited until he had seated himself before handing him the box. "Anything else?"

He shook his head, then locked the door, letting her pull it closed behind him. "Let's get out of here before someone stops us."

She stuffed the box into the back of the vehicle, once again looking around, feeling uncomfortable.

"Mr. Benson, is anyone after you for some reason?" She questioned Mark as she pulled out onto the street.

"Please make it Mark. And not that I know of. But I'm a forensics accountant and may have stirred something up somewhere along the line that I don't know about."

She nodded. "Then that's why we have someone following us all over the place?"

He turned to stare at her. "Following us?" He shot a glance over his shoulder, wincing as he did so. That wasn't such a good move, he thought.

"Yep! We picked them up at the hospital and they've been with us ever since."

He stared at her once more, then shook his head. "I have no idea who it would be. You're absolutely sure?"

"Absolutely. It's a dark grey car. I'll talk to Jason when we get back to my place."

"Jason?"

"My brother. He's on the force in town. He also works for me in his spare time. He's the one who'll be helping you as you need help."   She watched as the car closed the distance between them.

"What town did you say?   I don't remember either you or the surgeon saying."

She laughed.   "I don't think we did. It's the town your friend Josiah lives in, Elmton."

"Really?   Cool!"   He laid his head back, knowing they had about an hour's drive. His eyes slid closed and he slept.

Julia watched him for a few seconds before her eyes returned to the road. Okay, Lord, so why him? What's his need? You only send me people who are hurting and shattered. What do You need to heal in his heart?

The car following them sped up and around her, and she breathed a sign of relief. She hoped it just kept going. She didn't like the sense of danger she had felt since she met Mark.

❂ ❂ ❂ ❂

Julia turned as her brother approached and reached to grab some of the bags from the back of her vehicle, a smile lighting up her face.

21

"Any trouble? I thought you'd be back a bit earlier." Jason studied his sister's face, eyes narrowing at the stress he saw.

"A bit. I'll talk to you when I get Mark settled. He's not happy, Jason, and that's going to affect his recovery."

Jason held up the bags and then nodded towards the house. "Which room is he in?"

"The Willow Room. It has easier access to the porch and the ramp as he'll be in a wheelchair for the next couple of weeks anyway." She stopped, eyes troubled. "I think there's something more going on. We were followed today."

"Followed? How?" Jason was on alert, knowing his sister's safety could have been compromised.

Julia explained what she had seen and felt. Jason frowned, not liking this.

"It was after you picked up your new boarder?"

"It was. He said he felt something the day he was hurt. And someone messing with his office really threw him." Julia held the door for her brother and then followed him down the hall towards the room she had assigned Mark to. "Mark, this is my brother, Jason Long. You'll meet his wife, Maria, at supper."

Mark turned his chair from where he had been staring out the storm door and held out his hand. "Nice to meet you."

Jason stared at him as he set the duffel bags down. "I hear you've had some trouble following you."

Mark shrugged. "Maybe. I can't say for sure that we were followed, although your sister seems to think we were."

"If she says you were, you were." Jason's face had set into grim lines. "Get one thing straight. Julia's very observant and if she has noticed something off, then it is."

Mark stared between the two, not saying anything. Julia glared at him, then turned and walked rapidly away from the room. Jason watched her go, then turned his attention back to the man in the wheelchair.

"I think you need to get one thing straight here. Julia's been through a lot in her life, more than anyone should have to go through. If she says something is happening or she senses something, then it's right on. Her instincts have never failed her, or me. So, if you're going to be staying here, get used to that."

Mark sighed. "I'm sorry. I'm just not used to this."

"I get that, but you get this. Either you believe her or you don't. And if you don't, it could get both of you hurt. And if you hurt my sister, I'll deal with you myself."

Chapter 3

*W*iping the sweat from his forehead, Mark sat back down into his wheelchair. Julia was a hard taskmaster, but she knew her stuff.   His shoulder burned from the workout she had given him, geared to his healing ligaments.   She had warned him it would hurt and it had.

"Okay, Mark. I think that's enough for now.   Your shoulder is improving, much faster than I expected it to."   Julia approached him from where she had been putting way the equipment, an easy smile lighting up her face. "Tomorrow, you'll not be doing anything.   We always build rest days into your program."

"Have I really been here a week, Julia?" He grinned at her.

She nodded. "You have. The surgeon will be happy with your progress. I'll take you in next week and he'll take a look at both the shoulder and the leg." She stepped back to study his cast. "How's the pain level with the leg?"

"It's tolerable, I would say. I expected more pain. It's itchy though."

She laughed. "Yes, it will be. Hopefully next week, he'll be able to assess and see what type of cast is best suited." She handed him a bottle of water, then sank down on the bench near him. "Your room's been okay?"

"It's good. So are the meals. Maria's a good cook."

"She is. I've been blessed that she's been able to help." She stared off into the distance. "Have you been able to do any work?"

He nodded, then realizing she wasn't looking at him, spoke. "I have been. Thanks for putting in the wifi."

She nodded. "Our guests appreciate that." Her head turned as she heard a sound from outside. "I'll be back. There shouldn't be anyone around out there."

"Julia, wait. Let me come with you."

"And do what?" She disappeared from view into the office she had in the building.

Mark sat still for a minute, not quite sure if he should follow her, then sighed, and headed after her. The appearance of a man in the doorway stopped him.

"Where's Julia?" He tried to see around him to find her.

"Not your concern. You're the one I want."

"What? Why?" Mark was sure he had never seen this man before.

The man approached, then bent over to lean on the arms of the wheelchair. "You have something we want. And you're going to get it for us now."

Mark pushed backwards, sending the man off balance. "Who are you?"

The man laughed, a cruel sound in it. "Just get me what I want."

"I have no idea what it is. Where's Julia?" Mark was worried. Julia had not come back from the office. "What did you do to her?"

"Not your concern. I want that file."

"What file?" Mark was trying not to show the fear he felt, not just for himself. He knew something had happened to Julia and he needed to get into that office.

The man approached him once more, this time sending the wheelchair flying backwards until it hit the bench Julia had been sitting off. The chair tipped, spilling Mark to the floor, pain sending daggers through his left shoulder that he landed on. He slumped, not able to rise on his own, and the pain darkening his sight.

"Where is it?" The words hissed in his ear.

"I don't know what you want." Mark's sight faded and he didn't hear the man leaving, the sound of approaching footsteps driving him away.

Jason stopped at the doorway, looking for Julia, knowing she would be here. At the sight of Mark on the floor, Jason dropped the coffees he held and ran for him. On his knees, he assessed him, then called for the emergency services, his eyes scanning for his sister.

"Mark?"

Mark had started to move, pain wracking through his body. "Jason? What are you doing here?"

"I came looking for you two. What happened?"

"Some guy approached me, wanting a file he said I have. I have no idea what it is, though." He struggled to sit upright, Jason's hand helping him. "Where's Julia? She heard a noise in the office and headed that way. That's where he came from."

"Sit tight." Jason ran for the office, fear in his heart for his sister.

"Julia, where are you?" He reached for the light switch. Brightness filled the office and he frantically searched for her, finally finding her on the floor, her left arm and hand cradled in her right. He dropped beside her. "Julia? Wake up, hon. Julia?"

"Jason?" He heard one of his fellow officers calling.

"Tim, in here. Is someone with Mark?"

Tim appeared in the doorway. "Don is. What happened?"

"I don't know all of it yet. Mark said someone was looking for something he had. Julia came to see about a noise in here and didn't come back out." Jason stared down at his sister, his hand resting on her head. "Are the paramedics here?"

"Sue's heading this way with Ezra. Joe's with your boarder."

"Jason, what do we have?" Ezra stood beside him, his eyes watchful as Jason stood.

"Not quite sure yet. She hasn't moved since I found her."

Ezra dropped down to assess Julia, his comments quiet. Sue nodded as she headed back out to the ambulance.

"Ezra?" Jason waited for his attention. "What's going on?"

Ezra turned. "She was given a good blow to the head, Jason. It didn't break skin. But that's not our only concern." He didn't quite know how to tell his friend. His face darkened as he looked back down at Julia's hand. "She has some broken fingers, Jason. I'm not quite sure how that happened, given how she's lying."

"Broken fingers?" Jason stepped back, turning to stare out the door at Mark. "What kind of danger did he bring this way?" He was out of the office, heading for Mark when his name was called.

A fellow officer approached him. "The lieutenant from the county is heading in here. He'll want to take with you."

Jason blew out a frustrated breath, his attention going back to the office. He pointed at Mark. "Talk to him. Find out what he knows. Apparently whoever did this was wanted something from him."

Jason stood back in the doorway, watching as Ezra and Sue worked over his sister.

"How is she, Ezra?"

Ezra shook his head. "Still unconscious. She's got a couple of broken fingers, and as I said, that didn't happen with her fall. Not the bones that are broken and the way she fell."

Jason paled. "Are you telling me someone broke them?"

"It's possible." Sue spoke up. "We'll know more once an X-Ray has been taken."

Jason nodded. "I want to go with her."

Ezra turned to study him, then looked behind him. "Hello, Andrew."

Jason turned to the man standing behind, close in age to him. He didn't know the county police lieutenant very well. Andrew Scott had been tasked with leading the Elmton police force when the previous police chief had been arrested for murder and then murdered himself in a jail yard.

"Jason. Sorry about your sister. How is she?"

Jason shrugged. "She's unconscious. Ezra says she has some broken fingers and I gather he thinks that was done deliberately. Mark can give a description I think of who it was."

Andrew nodded, his body angled in such a way that he could see both places. "I know we've talked briefly about your sister. I'll come back to that. What about Mark?"

Jason stared at the man now seated in his wheelchair and watching him. "Julia said they were followed the day Mark came out here, that Mark thought his office had been searched. Mark also indicated that he felt something off the day he was hurt in his accident." Jason stopped, his eyes coming back to Andrew. "But did what happened to him constitute an accident or assault?"

Andrew drew in a deep breath. "I've talked to the patrol officer who responded. He felt that it was a deliberate attack but they found no evidence to support that. Mark had told him he thought something struck his bike wheel."

Jason's eyes slid closed. "And we brought him here to us."

Andrew shook his head. "We don't know what actually happened, Jason. He would be as safe here as anywhere. Julia made the decision to check out the office, right? Isn't that what happened? I know your sister. She'd walk right in without a second thought."

Jason turned as he heard a sound behind him, and watched as Mark was wheeled closer. He saw the bruises forming on his face and shuddered. If the assailant would do that to a man in a wheelchair, what more could he have done to a woman?

"Jason? How's Julia?" Mark's voice was quiet.

"She's unconscious still, Mark." He turned to watch as Ezra and Sue readied Julia on the stretcher to wheel her out. "She's also got some broken fingers. Deliberately broken fingers! Care to tell me now that you don't know anything?" Jason's fear for his sister fed his anger towards Mark.

Mark paled even more than he had been. "I have no idea, Jason. There's nothing that I'm working on that would warrant this."

Andrew spoke up, introducing himself. "Do you need to go and be seen to? No? Then, how about you and I head back to the house and have a chat. I need to know what's been going on and what you can tell me about what you do for employment."

Mark nodded, his eyes watching as Jason followed the stretcher.

"Jason?" He turned at Andrew's call. "Call me later and let me know how Julia is. I'll try and find you later if you don't. Tim's driving you over and staying with you."

"He's on duty at midnight." Jason protested.

"No.   He's on duty now, protecting Julia. I'll have Todd stay here with Mark. Until we determine what is going on, not one of you are by yourselves.   Got that?" Andrew held Jason's eyes until he nodded.

Chapter 4

Staring down at the mug of coffee he was twisting in his hand, Mark's thoughts were not on the questions he was being asked. They were instead on the woman lying in the hospital, hurt because of him. He sighed to himself. Not the way he wanted to impress her, he thought. And that's exactly what he was wanting to do. He had seen below her surface demeanour to the compassionate and caring woman and wanted to find out more about her. Not this way, Lord. I didn't want her hurt. Now, how do I fix this? He had no peace in his heart about this. He wanted to make it better and couldn't.

"Mark? Come back from where you are and talk to me." Andrew watched as Mark's eyes cleared and he looked at him.

"Sure. What was it you asked me?"

"What exactly do you do? I know you're an accountant."

"I'm a forensics accountant, hired to investigate financial portfolios and sometimes to track down financials for police organizations."

"Are you working on something right now that would have led to this?"

Mark shrugged. "I'm just starting a new investigation and haven't gotten that far into it, so I couldn't say. My past investigations shouldn't be a factor."

"Is this present investigation private or police?"

"It's private." Mark sat back in his chair, his eyes going to Andrew's. "It's strange, though. I've told you what Julia thought was happening. When we were in my office, things were moved around. Files weren't where I left them. I didn't see that anything was missing from any of them, but I can't guarantee someone didn't take copies of them."

"Do you normally lock your office?"

Mark shook his head. "No, none of us do. Though, come to think of it, I remember locking my desk and the filing cabinet before I left that night. Neither were locked when I stopped there that day."

Andrew nodded, his thoughts on what Mark had said. "What I would like to do is to have a detective go through your office with you, if we can? That way we can collect evidence if there's any there. Has the office been cleaned since you locked it?"

Mark shook his head. "If the office is locked, the cleaner moves on." Mark frowned. "I had the impression it had been freshly cleaned. It had just been done the night before I was hurt and wasn't to be done again for two weeks."

Andrew looked up from the notes he was making. "So, even if I have someone go through, they may not find anything. I'd still like that though."

Mark nodded. "Just let me know when." He sighed. "But I'll need transportation in."

"That's not a problem." He fished out his phone that was chiming. "Jason. Talk to me. How's Julia? I see. You're staying then, I take it? Tim's to stay with you both. I have someone here. Maria said she was headed for her Mom's, is that right? All right. Keep me updated. Listen, I need to get Mark to his office tomorrow. If Julia's up and around, let Tim stay with her. I would like you to go with Mark to meet a detective there. Yes, you. You're invested in this now."

Mark watched as Andrew pocketed his phone, then spoke. "Julia. How is she?"

Andrew sighed, just wishing this day had not happened. "She's still unconscious, but starting to rouse. Jason said she has a concussion." He paused, then continued, "X-Rays showed that she has two broken fingers on the left hand. Her physician has told Jason it was not from her going down. It had to be done deliberately, given the way they're broken."

"Deliberately?" Mark paled. "He did that to her on purpose? Because of me?"

"That's what we would surmise, Mark. Now, once again, is there anything you can tell me that would help me find this person?"

Mark shook his head. "There is nothing in my present investigation that would lead to this, not that I've been able to find yet. I can go through my past investigations, but no one comes to mind that would do this.”

Andrew nodded, then sighed. “This is not how I would have wanted today to end. It’s been one of those days and weeks.” He stood, his eyes watching as Mark pushed back from the table. “I have someone here with you tonight. Tomorrow, Jason will take you to your office where you’ll meet a detective from the force there. Be honest with us, Mark. It won’t be looked on with compassion if you’re not.”

Mark nodded. “I will.” He shuddered at the thought of how Julia was treated. “Maybe I should just pack up and go back to my place.”

“And do what? He knows you’ve been here. He’ll come back again and again until he gets what he wants, regardless of whether you are here or not. Jason’s picked up on your interest in his sister. If he has, you can be certain others have as well.”

Mark stared at him, a dumbfounded look on his face. “I was that obvious?”

Andrew shook his head, a smile crossing his face. “No, we just know how to read people better than most. Don't hurt her, Mark, or you'll have an entire force and town to deal with. She's been hurt enough in her life. We'd like to see her happy and content, and she hasn't been." He stopped, his eyes taking on a distant look. "Maybe you're the one the Lord has brought into her life. Maybe not. But as I said, don't hurt her heart."

Mark stared after Andrew as he walked away. I'm afraid I already have, Lord, and shattered it more than it was. What dreams has she lost because of what she's gone through? She needs healing, Lord. Please heal my friend.

✿ ✿ ✿ ✿

Jason stood in the doorway to Mark's office late the next morning, anxious to be back home. He had hated to leave when his sister was still in hospital, but he had had no choice. Andrew had been very specific about where he wanted him. He listened to the conversation between the detective and Mark, Mark struggling to make sense of what was going on.

"Jason, can you come in here for a second and close the door?" The detective,

41

Steve, Mark thought, asked him quietly. When Jason had closed the door, Steve turned back to Mark. "So, you're saying your desk and the filing cabinet were gone through but nothing was missing, just moved from place to place? Would anyone have done that if they were working on something assigned to you?"

Mark shook his head, a puzzled look on his face. "No, we each have our own client list. No one knows who we are working for or what we're working on. The way this office works is that we share office space and a receptionist, but we work independently."

Steve nodded, then crouched down to take a better look at the desk drawer lock. "It was tampered with, I can see that." He spun, searching the floor. "Here you go. Whoever it was missed this." Steve picked up a small slender piece of metal. "They used this to get into the drawer and likely into the cabinet as well. You don't have a computer here?"

Mark again shook his head. "Not here. I strictly use a laptop for work." He looked around, coldness running through him. "Is there any chance someone could be listening in to us?"

Steve shrugged. "It's always possible."

Jason spoke up. "Do you have much in here that you would need to pack?"

Mark turned to him, a question on his face. "Other than a bit of personal stuff in the drawer, just what's in the cabinet and this drawer."

Jason nodded, sharing a look with the detective. "Stay here. I'm going to go find some boxes. We're packing up your office and moving you out. Until we determine who and what, you're not coming back here."

Steve nodded. "About your phone, now. Do you use a phone here or your cell?"

"My cell. That's just how it works here. No phone system in our office if we don't want it."

Steve looked around once more. "I would definitely say someone tampered with your files. We have no way of knowing who now. I can test for prints, but I doubt I'd find any."

Mark turned to Jason as they headed back to Elmton. "What's this all about, Jason? You didn't pack me up just for the fun of it."

Jason shook his head. "No, we didn't. We'll need you to go through all those files and see if anything triggers a memory. That man yesterday was after something. He hurt my sister and I want him."

Mark nodded, not surprised at the vehemence with which Jason spoke. He would have felt the same. In fact, he did. Julia wasn't his sister, but she had become special to him in just that short week he'd known her. "I can do that, but don't be surprised if I come up with blanks."

"All we ask is if you find something, you give us permission to search further. If the person has been part of a police investigation, we can open the investigation up again."

Mark turned to stare out the side window, his mind going back over the cases he had handled, both now and in the past. "Have you heard how Julia is?"

Jason shot him a glance, one eyebrow raising. "Tim said she's home. Maria's got her comfortable in one of the rooms downstairs for now so she doesn't have to climb stairs."

"Jason, I can't tell you how sorry I am that she was hurt, probably because of me."

"It was because of you. We just need to find the creep that did it." Jason glanced at the rearview mirror and then down at the dash. He was driving just over the speed limit and the car behind was still approaching, too fast he thought. "What colour was that car that followed you? Dark gray?"

Mark nodded, shooting a glance out the back window. "He's back?"

Jason nodded. "It looks as if he is. Hang on. I'm going to try to lose him, but if it's your assailant, it won't make any difference."

Before Jason could make a move, the car had overtaken them and sped around them, passing close enough that Jason had to take evasive measures, finally coming to a stop on the side of the road.

Mark stared at him, eyes wide. "Did that really just happen?"

Jason nodded as he reached for his cell. "It did. I need to report this and then check in with Tim. I don't like that they're still around."

Mark sat back, his heart finally easing in its thundering as he calmed. *What is going on, Lord? Who is after me?*

Jason turned to Mark. "Julia's safe. Tim has called Andrew and is bringing in someone else. Maria's with her, so she's safe as well. So, once again, who is after you?"

Mark stared at him, his mind racing as to who it could be. "I have no idea. All this started when I took on my new client." He sighed, knowing he would have to give a name. "It's John Brown from your town. He's asked me to go over his financial portfolio. He's felt something off with it. So far, I haven't found anything, but I had only gotten started it on the day I had my accident. I felt something off, but it will take a lot of digging to find what it is, if it is hidden well."

Jason nodded. "I know John. He's honest and upright, but some of his family aren't. I can see why he's concerned." He stared out the window, fingers tapping the steering wheel, before he finally put the car in gear and drew back onto the asphalt. "We need to talk to Andrew and Bill, I think. Bill's a good friend and just made detective. He's like a bulldog with a bone, won't give up until he gets the answers he needs."

Chapter 5

Julia looked up at her brother as he stood, hands on his hips, staring down at her, a frown on his face.

"Julia, you're supposed to be resting." Jason was frustrated, to say the least, to find his sister at her desk, working.

"Jason, give it a rest. I need to do this paperwork or I won't get paid. I've done nothing but rest until about an hour ago. Go and ask Maria. She'll tell you. Now, get lost." She looked past him at Mark, sitting near her desk. "Go, Jason. I don't need you hovering over me like a mother hen."

"A mother hen?" Jason's voice rose in protest. "You've called me a lot of things over the years, but never a mother hen."

"Oh, yes I have. Now, go."

Jason shook his head and knowing he wouldn't win this battle, dropped a kiss on her head and went to find Maria. Mark watched him walk away, then turned back to Julia, to find her watching him

"How are you feeling, Mark? Was there any more damage done to the shoulder?"

Mark shrugged. "I didn't go and get it checked out. I was too worried about you."

She sat back, throwing her pen down. "That wasn't the smartest move you've made, now was it? That fall has likely set you back more."

"Actually, the shoulder feels way better this morning." He moved his arm and found the pain was better.

"That doesn't make sense. Unless.." Her voice faded away and she rose to approach him. "Where was the pain the worst?"

He pointed to the spot, and she touched it, then felt around the joint. "I would say that the fall likely pushed it back into proper place. The surgeon was concerned that the ligament damage might have keep it from moving the way it should." She stepped back, staring down at his leg. "Did the leg get hurt at all?"

He shrugged. "Not that I know of. Maria called the surgeon for me and he felt next week would still be okay but I was to go to the hospital here if I developed any new pain in it."

She nodded, then spun to pace. "Who was that, Mark? Who did this to me?" She held up her hand. "I need these to be able to work. I have to find someone to come in until I can." He could tell tears were near the surface.

"Julia, come, sit on the couch here." He moved back so she could walk by him and sit. He manoeuvred his chair over and then slid onto the couch beside her. "Jason and I cleaned out my office. I'm hoping doing that won't bring the man back here. I'd never forgive myself if you or Maria were hurt because of me."

"And if he does?" Julia's eyes never left his. "How do we really stay safe if you don't know who's after you?"

Frustrated, Mark nodded. "I know. I have to go back over the cases I've worked on, but I don't remember anything really standing out from them. It was the one I had just started. Something's off with the figures, and I hadn't got to the point where I needed to be. I've been trying to work on it for the last week, but haven't gotten anywhere."

Julia nodded, her eyes on her hands, not seeing the way Mark studied her face. She didn't quite know what to do with him. He was interested in her, she could tell, but she wasn't sure she would ever be ready for this.

"Mark, think. Is there anyone at all in your past before you started working as an accountant?"

He shook his head. "No, there isn't. Ask my friends. You know Josiah. Talk to him. We've been friends since high school."

"Really? That long?" Julia finally looked up at him.

He nodded and laughed. "That long. Listen, Julia. I don't want to put you or your family at risk. Maybe I should find somewhere else to stay."

"That won't work, Mark. He'll just follow you and someone else will get hurt."

She stared down at her fingers. "Living here, Jason's around and so are some of his buddies. Yesterday. Well, yesterday was yesterday."

Mark started to laugh, drawing her eyes to him and she frowned. "I'm sorry, Julia. That sounded so, how shall I say it, definite? Yes, yesterday was yesterday, and today's a new day. We need to move on." He tilted his head. "I see that smile."

She shook her head at him. "Mark, you're crazy, you know that? Back to what's going on."

He sobered. "What did that jerk say to you?"

"Jerk? Wow, descriptive aren't we today?" She grinned at him as he shook a finger at her. "What did he say? I can't remember him saying much other than asking where you were. I didn't get a chance to say anything before he did this?" She held up her hand. "Then, I don't remember what happened."

Mark nodded, knowing this had likely been the case. "Do you remember anything about him?"

"Other than I was scared stiff?" She shuddered, then shook her head. "It happened too fast and the lighting was dim in the office. You likely had a better chance of seeing something about him."

"Yeah, well, I didn't really. I was too worried about you." Mark watched as she raised her eyes to him, a puzzled look on her face. "Yeah, I was really worried. I don't want you hurt because of me."

She turned her gaze from him to stare out the window behind the couch. She swallowed hard before she looked back at him, an uncertain look in her eyes. "Mark, please don't go there. Just get yourself well so you can move back home."

He shook his head. "Too late, Julia. I want to find out who you are and what makes you tick. I also really like this town. Jason's been looking for a place for me. I'm ready to move out of Logan City, have been for months."

She stared at him, then rose to pace back to her desk. She seated herself, her eyes on her paperwork, and then picked up her pen, trying to concentrate on what was before her. She finally sighed, and laid down her pen. "Mark. I understand what you're saying, but I...I.." She rose and almost ran from the room, Mark's eyes following her in consternation.

He reached for his wheelchair and moved to follow her, finding Jason in the doorway.

"What did you say to her? You've made her cry and I warned you." Jason looked angry as he walked forward into the room.

Mark's hand went up. "Other than I wanted to get to know her better and that I wanted to move to this town to live, nothing. What's going on, Jason? I know something is."

Jason studied the man in front of him for moments, then finally sighed, sinking down into an armchair. "I guess I need to talk to you." He rose again and shut the door to the room, knowing that would signal he didn't want to be disturbed. "You're new to town. You don't know Julia's history or mine." Jason paused, running his hands through his hair. "Where do I start without making Julia feel like I betrayed her?"

"What is public knowledge that you can share? Or is anything? I can see the concern of a big brother in there."

"There is." Jason sat, eyes brooding, a faraway look on his face. "Julia and I share a mother, not a father. My Dad was killed in the line of duty as a police officer. My Mom married again about two years later to Julia's Dad. I was never once made to feel any less than I was Mac's son and to all intents and purposes I was. I was only one when Dad was killed, so I don't have any memories of him. That puts about four years between us.

"Julia was never a daredevil, always thinking of the consequences of any action she took. Until she met Dominic. He changed her into someone we didn't know. She became reckless. Dad and Mom tried to talk to her, but she refused to listen. She and Dominic had planned to elope when she was 17, we found out after the fact, but on the way out of town, they were in a serious car accident. Dominic was high on drugs and Julia didn't know he used. He hid that from her. He was killed and she was badly hurt. That changed her from the sunny cheerful girl we knew to what you see today. Something else happened at that time she's never ever talked about." Jason rose to pace.

Mark looked down at the floor, his thoughts following the words Jason had spoken. "She's never said?"

Jason shook his head. "No, she hasn't. Something scare her more than just the accident. She refused to talk about it then and still today won't say a word." He turned. "When you were talking to her, I was in the hall. I wasn't meaning to eavesdrop, but I did. Forgive me. I heard the old Julia there for a moment. I want to thank you for that. I know you made her cry, but we haven't seen her cry for anyone since the accident. Not Dad. Not Mom. No one."

Mark nodded. "I'll do what I can to help, Jason. I'm just afraid that I'll bring harm to her."

Jason snorted. "You already did, man. Just make sure you don't bring any more." He paused, a thought gathering in his mind. "Any more word on what we were talking about?"

Mark shook his head. "No. I have to speak with the portfolio holder. I'm hoping

I can meet with him soon, as in the next day or so. I just have to find a driver to take me there."

"Julia or I will. Just let us know." Jason stood and opened the door. "Come on. Maria has supper ready for us."

Chapter 6

Julia stared at the house she had just stopped in front of and then at Mark. "You really are going to meet with him?"

"I am. Any reason I shouldn't?"

She shook her head. "No. I'm just surprised you're ready to meet with him already, given that yesterday you hadn't found anything."

He nodded. "I know. I usually meet with a client once I start, just to ask more questions and see what else they can give me. This time it's difficult though." He stared down at his leg. "How am I supposed to get up the stairs?"

"We'll go around back. The ground is level and they have a patio back there. Once I get you set, I'll go find him."

Mark nodded, then reached for the door. "I'll be glad when I'm mobile again.

What day do I have to see the surgeon? It's not soon enough, I tell you."

Julia laughed, her smile lighting up her face. Mark stared at her, wanting to make that happen more and more. What was she dealing with, Lord?

"Tuesday. We'll get you there, it's not that long away." She pushed his wheelchair around to the back of the house. "Sit tight. I'll be right back."

Mark stared around at the backyard of the house he had come to. It was well laid out, but something just seemed off. He shivered, finding he felt watched. He turned to look at the back of the house, catching a curtain as it dropped back into place. Okay, Lord, so what's going on?

"Mark. Good to see you again." John Brown reached to shake his hand. "Good to see you're up and around."

"I'm getting there. I just wanted to update you on your portfolio you brought me." He looked past the older man to where Julia stood, waiting. "It won't take long, though." He went through what he had found so far, John's eyes following him.

John sat back, sighing. "I hear what you're not saying, Mark. You're one of the best, highly recommended to me. I know you're going to keep digging until you get the answers we need. Just stay safe, okay? I heard what happened to you and Julia. If it's because of me, I…"

Mark's raised hand stopped him. "The police don't have enough evidence to suggest that. We're looking into more cases than yours."

John nodded as he stood, his eyes suddenly glinting with mischief. "I'm glad you're here in town. We need more residents like you. That young lady behind me, she could use someone to make her smile all the time. I think you're the one." He shook Mark's hand and walked away, stopping to say something to Julia that made her laugh and drew her eyes to Mark.

Julia approached him, a question in her eyes. "What did John say to you at the end?"

Mark shook his head, smiling. "Someday, maybe I'll tell you. What did he say to you?"

She gave a small smile. "Just something I've never heard him say before. Let's get you out of here. I feel like there's evil around here somewhere."

He nodded. "I felt like that as well. Do you have clients today?"

"I do, but I've had a friend come in to cover for me until I can get back to working. This is just so frustrating."

He nodded. "I know. So, what do we do with the rest of the day? I can work at any time, and I find late at night is when I concentrate best. It's quieter than and has less distractions." He grinned at the look she threw me.

"I'm a distraction, am I?"

Mark smiled and reached to lay his hand on her arm. "You are and in the best possible way."

She stared at him, her mouth open until he tapped her chin to close it. "Mark!"

He grinned. "It's the truth. Isn't that what we agreed to ?"

She shook her head as she came to a stop at the traffic lights. "So, then what do you want to do for today?"

He shrugged. "I'm open to suggestions. What do you suggest?"

"Lunch first. I'll pop into the cafe and grab us something. I know a place where you'll be able to get around in your chair."

An hour later, Mark folded up the wrapper from his sandwich and stared around. Julia had brought him to a quiet park, overlooking the lake outside of town.

"This is a nice area."

Julia nodded, her eyes searching the area. She didn't feel safe here today, not like she usually did. This was the place she came to, to think, to ponder God's word, to ask for guidance.

"It is, but for some reason, it doesn't feel safe today."

He nodded. "I get the same feeling." He looked towards the parking lot as a vehicle pulled in. "Didn't you say no-one came here?"

"I did. I don't like this, Mark."

"Nor do I. Let's head for your car."

Halfway there, they stopped, eyes watching the three men walking towards them.

"Mark?"

"I know, Julia. They're hiding their faces. Where's your phone?"

"In the car. Where's yours?"

"At your place." He watched the men walk closer. "This isn't good."

The men stopped, one standing in front of them, two going behind them.

The first one spoke. "We don't want to hurt you. We just want to speak with you."

"About what?" He reached for Julia's hand and clasped it tight in his.

"We need to go somewhere we can talk where we won't be seen. My friends will help you into our vehicle."

"Now, wait a minute. We're not going anywhere with you." Mark made to rise from his chair, but hands behind him on his shoulders kept him down.

Julia smothered a scream as she was forced away from Mark and to the vehicle, parked in such a way that she couldn't see a license plate. Mark was pushed towards the van as well. The men stepped up behind them, blindfolds in their hands.

"I'm sorry, Julia, Mark, that we need to do this. It's for your own protection."

Julia shared a look with Mark, then blindfolded, allowed herself to be helped into the van. Mark landed on the seat beside her, reaching for her hand. She clutched his, his grip strong and steady, letting her draw from his strength. She tried to trace their route, but couldn't, there were just too many twists and turns in it.

Finally, the vehicle stopped and they were pulled from it, Mark held steady as he was helped to a chair. Julia reached for his hand once again from where she sat beside him in a building.

They could hear movement around them, and then the blindfolds were removed. Blinking, they both looked around. Julia frowned. Didn't she know this place, she thought, then mentally shrugged. Jason would likely be able to figure it out.

"What do you want with us?" Mark went on the offensive, but got no response from the man standing in front of them, the other men standing behind them. They heard a door open and knew someone else had entered, but he or she didn't say a word.

Mark watched at the silent communication going on around him and over his head. He took a quick look at Julia, who sat there, a puzzled look on her face. She glanced at him, then back at the man in front of her.

"What do you want?" Mark repeat.

The man nodded, then looked at Mark. "You're a stranger to our town, but not a stranger to what you do. We need your assistance. We have members in our community who are struggling with financial details, who are being used by criminals to laundry money. We need you to help us catch them."

"Go to the police."

The man shook his head. "We can't; at this point, we don't have enough evidence to warrant an investigation. If word got out that's what we had done, the criminals would pack up and move to another town. They've done this before and gotten away with it. We want to stop it here and now."

Julia shared a look with Mark. "How do we help you?"

"We will provide Mark here with the information and portfolios we need him to go over. Don't worry. We've retrieved them legitimately. We ask that he investigate them and let us know what he finds. We will set up a secure email contact that doesn't trace to either one of us that we will contact him on in the future"

"And if I refuse?" Mark was not backing down, not when he had Julia to consider.

"Then, our conversation is over. We deliver you back to Julia's vehicle and you are free to go on your way."

"Do I have to decide now?"

The man nodded. "You do. Either you're working with us or not."

Julia stared at him as he considered the man's words. He sighed, knowing he would have to help. It just wasn't in him not to.

He nodded. "I'll help, but I want Julia to stay clear of it."

The man shook his head. "She knows the people in her town. She can help you with this. Unfortunately, it does come with risk." He nodded at the two men behind them, then waited as the door closed behind the fourth man, who walked away, pulling down the hoodie he had raised before entering the cabin.

Later that day, Mark looked up from the paperwork he had spread out on the kitchen table, Maria working around him. Julia stood watching him.

"How's it going, Mark?"

He pointed at a chair and waited until she had seated herself. "It's going. I'm finding out some information on that call we made this morning"

She looked up at Maria, then back at him. "You have? Progress, I like that. Tomorrow, you'll be back doing physio."

He looked up at that and then pointed at her hand. "And just how are you planning on doing that?"

She smirked. "I'm not. Paulie will be. He's a harder taskmaster than I am."

"Great. Just what I need."

"Clear your paperwork please, Mark." He looked up to see Maria standing beside him. "I need to be setting the table for supper."

He nodded and gathering the paperwork, headed for his room, hearing the quiet conversation behind him.

"Julia." When Julia didn't look up, Maria started at the ceiling, then spoke again in a louder voice. "Julia."

Julia jumped at the sound in Maria's voice. "Yes?"

"Just what is going on? You disappear with Mark this morning and come back looking really shaken. That's not you. Nothing shakes you. Then I find him with paperwork spread out all over and you two are talking in a cryptic manner." She raised her eyes to see Jason standing in the doorway and shook her head. He nodded and moved away.

Julia shrugged, not sure how to answer or how much to answer.

Maria sat down beside her and reached for her hands. Julia was the sister she had never had and always wanted. She was also a dear friend. "Julia. Talk to me."

Julia stared across the kitchen, a distressed look on her face. "I can't, Maria. I can't tell you what's going on. I made a promise not to."

"And does it involve Mark?"

Julia nodded. "It does." She bit her lip, not quite sure how to proceed, and sighed. "It's too dangerous to tell you, Maria, and I know Jason will be very angry if he knows." She missed Maria's look over to the doorway where Jason stood once again, a frown on his face. Maria watched as Jason disappeared, knowing he was going to find Mark.

Jason tapped at Mark's door, watching as Mark tidied up his paperwork.

"Jason? I don't like that look on your face." Mark sat back in his chair, wishing he could stand and face the brother of the woman he was really interested in getting to know better.

"Talk to me, Mark. Tell me what went down today."

"What do you mean?"

"I heard Julia say something to Maria and I want to know what's going on." Jason sank down on the edge of the bed, eyes fastened on Mark.

Mark sighed. "I wish I could tell you, Jason, but at the moment, I don't have enough information to even begin to figure out what's going on."

"So what is?" Jason was not going to let him get away with that cryptic statement.

Mark shook his head. "It's something that involves people in your town." Mark stopped, eyes tracing to the outdoors. "Have you ever suspected that you have dishonest people in your town?"

Jason snorted. "What town doesn't? Now, hold on. Wait a minute! Are you suggesting the bank is dishonest?"

Mark shook his head, eyes fastened on Jason's. "Not the bank, not directly."

Jason stared at him, a dawning look coming over his face. "I get you now. I know what you're investigating. It has nothing to do with what you were working on, has it?"

Mark shrugged. "So far, I haven't been able to spend enough time on that. These investigations can take weeks or months."

Jason stood. "It hadn't better take that long, Mark. Maria has supper ready. Be prepared to keep me informed every step of the way. I don't want to see Julia hurt."

"Nor do I."

Jason stopped at the tone in Mark's voice and turned back to him. "Something you want to share with me?"

Mark smiled, shaking his head. "Not yet."

"Just don't get her hurt or hurt her yourself. You'll have more than me to deal with if you do."

"Gotcha. I'll do my best. God willing, He'll protect her."

Chapter 7

*J*ulia watched as Mark walked towards her, leaving the wheelchair behind. A grin on his face said it all.

"No more wheelchair?"

He shook his head. "The surgeon was really pleased with how it was healing, considering our adventure last week. What he hadn't told me at the time was that it wasn't a complete break, which makes it a shorter healing time. He thinks another two weeks and I can ditch the cast."

She smiled. "That's wonderful news. God has been good in healing you. That means you won't have to have much physio on it. What about the shoulder?"

"He's happy with it as well. He doesn't think I'll need much more on it either." He stopped, a sadness coming over his face. "But if I don't that means I'll be needing to find another place to live."

Julia shook her head. "Not necessarily. You can stay with us until you figure out where you want to be. Jason and Maria don't mind you around."

"Are you sure?" He searched her face, looking for an answer to a question he wasn't ready to ask.

"We are. We talked about it last night. Jason said to make sure you knew you could stay."

Mark stared out the window of the car, then shot a glance behind him. "Isn't that car a little close?"

"It is. I need to get away from him and there isn't a spot along here to do that." She braced herself as the car rammed them from behind, throwing her steering off. "Hang on, Mark. I can't control us."

The car slid across the road, landing on the opposite shoulder before she could stop it. The car that had hit them stopped in front of them, and two men from it approached them.

"Is your door locked?" Mark's voice had a hint of his fear.

"They are.   Unless they break the glass, they can't get in. I've already sent a text to Jason."

The men tried the doors, and then banged on the windows.   A weapon appeared in one man's hand.

"What do we do, Mark? They'll shoot us if we don't open the door!"

"I know."   He threw up his hands as the back passenger window shattered and he ducked the flying particles of glass.   The weapon jabbed at the back of his head.

"Unlock the door or she dies!"

Julia gave a small scream at the sound of more gunfire and the window behind her blew out.   The glass knocked out, a hand reached beside her and unlocked the door. Her seatbelt unclipped, she was dragged from the car and a weapon held to her head.

"I would suggest you cooperate, Benson. Otherwise, your girlfriend dies."

Mark released his seatbelt, and shoving open his door stood, his eyes glued to Julia. What have we gotten into, Lord? How do we get out of here?

They were shoved to the car and then inside.   Mark reached for Julia's hand, holding it tight as she moved as close to him as she could. Eyes watchful, Mark frowned, trying to place the men. He had never seen them before that he knew. So, why did they want him?

Finally, the car turned into a narrow bumpy leading to a one-story house with a barn behind it. He heard Julia gasp and shot her a quick glance.   She shook her head, distress on her face. Whose place was it, he wondered?

Yanked from the car, they were pushed into the house and then into an interior room with no windows. The door locked behind them and darkness descended.

Mark stood, gathering his breath, listening. He could hear Julia near him.

"Julia?" He turned and moved, finally catching her hand. He pulled her into his arms. "What just happened?"

She leaned her forehead against him. "We were kidnapped, you think? By who?"

He gave a small smile she couldn't see. "You seemed to know this house?"

He felt her nod. "It's passed through so many owners, I don't know who owns it now. Your client, Brown, it used to be his father's."

"Brown? It comes back to him? Why doesn't that surprise me?"

"What is going on with that, anyway?" She moved away from him, and he could hear her pacing the room.

"I have no idea." He turned as the door opened and bright light shone in, blinding them.

"You'll have two hours, Benson, to agree to our demands. If you don't, your girlfriend disappears for good." The door slammed and they were once more in darkness.

"Mark?" He could hear the fear in her voice and searched until he found her, wrapping her close once more. "We need to come up with a plan, but right now, I don't see what we can do."

Mark nodded as he shuddered inside. How was he to get her out of here? He had no information that he could or would pass on about his client. He just hadn't found it.

He sighed, laying his head down on hers. "We pray, Julia. We pray that someone comes. Other than that, I have no plan. I don't have anything I can give them."

She nodded. "That's that, then, isn't it?"

❁ ❁ ❁ ❁

Jason braked hard and throwing the car in park, was out and over to Andrew's side. He bent to look at Julia's car and cringed.

"Andrew?"

Andrew turned to Jason. "Someone got to them, Jason. Why didn't she tell us she had to come in here and let us have someone with her?"

Jason shook his head. "She's too independent to do that. I've tried to get her to work with us, but she's refusing. Now both of them are gone."

Andrew nodded. "There's no blood in the car or around it, so we're assuming they're alive and unhurt. But where did they get to?" He turned to Jason. "Would she have her cell on her or in her purse?"

Jason stared at him, then back at the car. "Is her purse inside?"

Andrew nodded, then walked over to the tech working around the car. "Have you bagged her purse?"

He nodded and handed it to her. "Wallet, brush, some candies, tissues, pen, pad of paper, a file of business cards. No phone."

"And it's nowhere in the vehicle?"

"Not that we see. If you call it, maybe we can find it."

Andrew shook his head. "I don't want to do that, just in case she has it with her." He turned back to Jason. "No phone. And I would hazard a guess Mark has his with him."

Jason nodded. "I would think so. Now what?"

Andrew turned in a circle, scanning the area. "They picked a good place to ambush them. From what I'm told, they were hit from behind and likely pushed across the road. Julia did a good job stopping her car."

Jason nodded. "That's no consolation when they're missing." He reached for his phone as it chimed. "It's Julia. She's able to send a text. How?"

Andrew leaned close to read it. "The old Brown place? Do you know where it is?"

Jason paced. "There are just too many places the Browns owned. Can we trace her cell?"

"We can try."

❂ ❂ ❂ ❂

The door to the room slammed open and two of men stood there.

"Where is it?"

"Where's what?" Mark shoved Julia behind him.

"The cell phone. We know you have them on you."

Mark lifted his hands. "What makes you think that?"

Mark was shoved against a wall and his phone tugged from his pocket. He heard a whimper from Julia and spun, lunging

79

towards the man reaching for her phone. He wrestled with him to get him away from her as her phone spun out of her hand and broke on the floor. Mark felt himself lifted and then thrown towards a wall, sliding down it to land in a heap. Julia stared at the men, tears of fright in her eyes, not knowing what was happening, before the door slammed shut again.

Kneeling by where she knew Mark lay, she reached for his face. Please, Lord, let him be alive. She sank back against the wall, cradling Mark to her, not knowing what would happen now. She swiped at the tears on her face, but couldn't stop them falling.

✪ ✪ ✪ ✪

Jason walked towards Andrew, stern lines carved in his face. He touched Andrew's shoulder and motioned him away from the other officers.

"Something's happened to Julia's cell. The text messages aren't going through."

Andrew stopped, his heart dropping. "Were you able to get one out to her?"

Jason shook his head. "No. Between the time I got hers and could try to send one, that's when her phone went dead."

Andrew nodded. "So, the battery's either dead or they've discovered them."

"I would say they found the phones. Something tells me it wasn't an accident either. Someone's watching us right now, Andrew, and passing on what we're doing."

"I know. I get that feeling too." He sighed and then leaned back on his car. "I don't like this, Jason. Do you have any idea where they might be?"

Jason shook his head. "Not really. Brown's father owned about 30 places hereabouts. He had been into real estate. The family sold them off once he passed away, just keeping the ones they wanted to live in themselves."

"So we either go to Brown, or we start a search."

"I already have. I called a friend to start that. Samuel's a title searcher and can find the information quicker than we can."

Andrew nodded. "Good. Now are there any places you can think of that are out of the way?"

Jason sighed. "They had about 15 that were in the country, and I can't remember where they all were. I was too young."

Chapter 8

Julia held a hand up to block the light pouring into the room. She was hauled to her feet and dragged from the room. Mark was dragged behind her, she could tell, his feet not working as they should and he stumbled many times. Shoved into a different vehicle, she wondered where they were heading to now. Mark slumped beside her, his head falling over on her shoulder. What did they do to you, Mark, she wondered?

Blindfolded once more, Julia grasped Mark's hand, feeling the limpness in his. How badly was he hurt, she wondered? What seemed like hours later but not likely was, the vehicle stopped and they were once more pulled from it and shoved forward. Mark's feet were working better and he kept a firm grasp on Julia's hand.

Shoved down onto a hard chair, Mark listened for sound or movement around him. Hearing nothing, he reached for his blindfold, his hands stopping as he felt a nudge in the back of his head. Not alone, he thought. *Lord, I have no idea what's going on. But couldn't You have gotten my attention a little easier? I know. We're in a battle You've already won. I just don't see the victory here.*

Footsteps finally sounded as men entered the room. No, make that a woman as well. The footsteps sounded different. He heard a whimper from Julia and tried to move towards where he heard her but was shoved back into his chair.

"Mr. Benson. It's time we came to an understanding." The low voice was hoarse. "We want the information you have been asked to investigate."

Mark shook his head. "I don't have anything that is yours. The investigation hasn't even started any way. Who are you?" He felt the metal on the back of his head again, and his thoughts swirled. *How do I get us out of here?*

"That's too bad, Mr. Benson. We really wanted your cooperation. You've made your decision. We've made ours."

He turned as he heard a low cry from Julia. "Don't hurt her." He was out of his chair, hands reaching for his blindfold as he lunged towards Julia.

Julia screamed as she heard a body hit the floor. Mark, what did you do? She was pulled from her chair and out of the room, out of the house, and shoved once more into a vehicle, one of her captors on either side of her. She struggled to get past them, clawing at their arms until her wrists were bound. A voice finally penetrated her fog of fear.

"If you continue to struggle, he dies. Behave yourself and he may yet live."

Her head turning, she frowned. She knew that voice but who was it? Defeated she slumped back, her thoughts racing as she tried to come up with a plan.

⊙ ⊙ ⊙ ⊙

Andrew paced through the abandoned house, his eyes on the scuff marks in the dust. He could see that Mark had been here, just by the track of the walking cast. He stopped, peering around him, then walked towards the centre of the house.

"Andrew?" Jason appeared in the doorway of the house, unsure whether to enter or not.

"Come on in, Jason. The team's been and gone." Andrew looked up at the younger man, seeing the strain and stress showing in his face.

"They were here?'

Andrew nodded. "Mark was for sure, and I'm guessing Julia was too. It's hard to tell from the footprints, though, they just cover one another."

Jason stared around, then headed to check out each room. "Which room were they in?"

"That one." Andrew pointed, then followed Jason. "There's some blood on the lower wall, so one of them was hurt. I'm guessing it was Mark, trying to protect your sister."

"Who did this, Andrew?" Jason turned tortured eyes to his superior.

"We're working on it, Jason." He turned to glance behind him at a sound and then disappeared from Jason's view.

Jason spun in a circle, studying the room. Where are you, Julia? I promised Dad I'd keep you safe and I haven't.

"Jason?"

Jason headed toward Andrew's voice. "Yes, Andrew?"

"We've got word that one of the patrols have found Mark and is heading in with him to Emerge. No sign of Julia. I'm sorry."

Jason drew a deep breath, his face whitening at the news. "So, then, where is she?"

"The officer said it looks as if she had been there and then taken away. Mark was found unconscious."

Jason nodded. "I'm not on duty. I'm heading that way, then."

Andrew stopped Jason with a hand to his arm. "Jason, I don't have to tell you to be very cautious. I don't want this investigation compromised in any way."

Jason stood, eyes staring straight ahead, a shuttered grim look on his face. He turned his tortured eyes to Andrew and nodded. "Don't worry. I won't impede the investigation or compromise it. I just want my sister home."

Andrew nodded. "We all do. Now, go. See what Mark can tell you. I have the team headed to where he was found."

Jason stepped forward, then stopped, his back stiff. "Was it another one of Brown's houses?"

Andrew shot him a look, then looked down at the address he had been given. "No, not this time. This time the title is registered to a numbered company. Listen, let me have the name of your friend, the one who's a title searcher. I'll have him run it for us, to see what he can find."

❂ ❂ ❂ ❂

Jason stood at the window in Mark's hospital room, his eyes staring out but not seeing anything, stern lines carved into his face. Where are you, Julia, he thought? Where is she, Lord? I pray she's still alive. Please, Lord, don't take her from me. I can't handle that. He turned at a sound from the bed, and leaning back against the window, crossed his arms, eyes on Mark as he roused.

Mark's eyes fluttered open and closed, his hand finding the sore spot on his head. Where was he? Julia! Where was she? He sat upright, then sank back against the pillows as shards of pain shot through him. He closed his eyes and waited for the room to stop spinning in circles.

Jason pushed away from the wall to stand beside the bed, hands grasping the side rail. He watched as Mark tried to come out of the darkness he was in and failed. Jason sighed, looking up at the wall ahead of him, then turning as the door opened and Andrew stood there.

"Has he been awake yet, Jason?"

Jason shook his head. "Not fully, just kind of rousing now and then." He turned to Andrew again. "Any news?" His heart sank at the negative shake of Andrew's head. "Where is she?"

"God knows, Jason."

Jason pushed away from the bed, anger in his movements. "Platitudes, Andrew? I know that but it doesn't help, now does it? I just want my sister home, safe and sound."

Andrew remained silent, his eyes following Jason as he paced, then returned to watch Mark.

Mark roused, his eyes opening and blinking as he stared around, a frown on his face as he tried to concentrate. He scrubbed at his face, wincing as he hit the temple area and the large bandage covering it.

"Mark?"

A voice from the side caught his attention, and he turned, eyes shutting against the pounding in his head.

"How are you, Mark?"

"Jason?" At the affirmative answer, he lay back on the pillows, eyes still shut. "Sounds as if a blacksmith has taken up residence with his anvil and hammer. How are I supposed to feel after getting hit over the head?"

"Andrew's here as well. He'd like to ask you some questions."

Mark gave a brief nod, then cracked his eyes open to watch as Andrew stood at the foot of the bed. "I have no idea who they were, Andrew. All they said was that they wanted the information I was working on." He tried to sit, and stopped as his head spun.

Jason found the button and raised the head of the bed, Mark nodding his thanks, then handed him the glass of water sitting on the table beside the bed.

"Walk me through what you can remember, Mark." Andrew watched, an unreadable look in his eyes. "Start from when you were hit."

Mark stared at Andrew. "We were hit? I don't remember that at all. I don't remember much other than them wanting what I was working on. I can't even remember where we were or what day it is."

"Did you see any faces, recognize any voices?"

Mark started to shake his head and stopped at the pain. "No, I didn't, but I'm not from here. I wouldn't know who they were."

"Are you saying they're from town?"

Mark turned to stare at Jason. "That's the impression I got. Julia may have recognized them." He stopped, staring between the two men as they exchanged grim glances. "Wait a minute. What haven't you told me? Where's Julia?" He threw back the blankets and fumbled for the side rail, trying to put it down.

Jason sighed, his hand going to Mark's shoulder to keep him in bed as he pulled the blankets back up. "You're not going anywhere, Mark. The doctors will tie you to the bed if you try to get up. You have a fairly severe concussion there. It looks as if you have had a couple of powerful blows to the head."

Mark laid back, his eyes tracing the ceiling tiles. "I wouldn't know. I don't remember much after the first one. But, where is Julia?"

"That we don't know, Mark. We were hoping you could tell us."

Mark brought his eyes back to Andrew. "If I could, I would. I have no idea where she is." He stared past Andrew at the open door, a frown coming over it as he saw the man again, the one who had been at his hospital door all those weeks ago. "Who's that man?"

Andrew spun and headed for the door, motioning for Jason to stay where he was.

"What's going on, Mark?"

"That man. He's the same one who was there before." He looked up at Jason before back at Andrew as he came into the room again. "Who is he?"

Andrew and Jason shared a look. "He was gone when I got out there, mingling somehow with the people in the hall. I'll have a sketch artist come by tomorrow and see what you can come up with." He raised a hand at Mark's protest. "I understand you're not going home for a couple of days. So stay put and work with us."

Chapter 9

*T*wo weeks later, Mark threw the paperwork he was searching through onto the table in the living room, running his hands through his hair. He just didn't see what he needed to see. He rubbed blurry eyes and rose, heading for the kitchen and more coffee.

Maria turned as she heard him and pointed at the table. "Sit, Mark. You need to eat."

He shook his head as he refilled his mug and set the carafe back on the burner. "I can't, Maria. I just can't."

"No, you can. You just won't. Starving yourself won't bring Julia home. She'd be the first one to tell you to sit and eat." Compassionate brown eyes watched as Mark finally nodded and sat. "Here, try this soup and bread. If you don't eat, you'll end up back in the hospital and that won't help anyone."

He nodded. "I know, Maria. I know. I just can't find what I want in all that paperwork. Whoever I'm after has hidden it well."

"Let me take a look. Fresh eyes may help." Maria looked up at Jason standing behind Mark. "Let Jason and I help you."

He finally looked up, a bleakness on his face. "I have talked to Brown. He said to bring in who I needed. There's just something I can't put my finger on." He started to rise. "Let me get the paperwork."

"Sit, Mark. I'll get it." Jason headed for the living room and gathered up everything Mark had there. "Where do we start?" he asked as he dropped it onto the table. "Where are your notes?"

"Notes? I haven't written anything down. I don't usually."

Jason shook his head as he rose and headed for the home office, coming back with paper and tape. Maria rose to help him as they tacked it up on the kitchen wall. "This is how we work a case, Mark. We have whiteboards at work, but this will have to do for now. Whenever we come across something, it goes down here. Maria, do we have lots of sticky notes?"

"That we do. Julia had stocked up, buying way more than she needed. Let me get them." She came back, hands full. "She loves the coloured ones. Good thing. We can use that to our advantage." She help up her laptop as well. "I'll transfer this to a program on here as well. That way, when we take down that, we'll still have a copy to work with."

Mark sat back, staring at the two. "Now, why didn't I think of that?" He sighed, his eyes growing distant. "I just wish this hadn't happened, that I hadn't met Julia."

Jason and Maria exchanged a glance before Jason spoke. "Mark, don't think like that. This could have happened at any time, with anyone. God has a plan and purpose we don't see. Just work with us, okay? Julia would not want you to talk like this."

"Like what?" Mark shoved back from the table, catching his chair before it fell. "I brought this to her. No one else."

Maria watched as he paced in an agitated manner, her heart raised in prayer. "Mark." When he didn't respond, she rose and stood in his way, causing him to stop and stare down at her. "Mark, listen to us. Now sit."

Mark gave a half-smile. "You make it sound like I'm a dog. That's twice you've said, Mark, sit." And he did just wanted she had ordered him to do.

Maria laughed, the sound breaking through the tension in the kitchen, sliding back into her own chair and reaching for Jason's hand. "I'm going to talk to you like I would to my own brother. And yes, I can see where you and Julia are headed, even if you two are too blind to see it yourself."

Mark nodded. He had an older brother and he knew exactly what Martha would be saying to him, let alone his mother or father. "Okay, so what is it? Don't give me some generic form of what God says or is planning or is doing. I can do that myself."

She stared at him, her head tilted to the side. Her red hair was caught back into a braid. "Okay, then I won't. Let me talk straight to your heart, then. I've seen how you and Julia are dancing around one another. Julia's been hurt and hurt badly in the past. Part of it was her own doing, part of it someone else's. Some of the town judged her and caused her to withdraw from just about everyone. I have seen her open up to you in a way she hasn't to anyone other than Jason or myself. You're bringing her back to where she was." She paused, biting at her upper lip. "She has a lot of shattered dreams, Mark, shattered by the actions of others. She didn't want to be a physiotherapist. What she really wanted was to be a photographer, wanted to travel the world and find those pictures no one else could find. That can't happen now because of injuries she suffered years ago. Those injuries drove her to her work today."

Mark nodded, then looked at the paper on the wall. "I get that, Maria. I really do. We all have had dreams we've lost and let go." He pointed to the wall. "We need to find out what's going on, or I'm afraid we won't see her again."

Jason rose three hours later, his phone in his hand. "Andrew, what do you have? I see. Another dead end, then? What aren't you saying? I know. I know. Mark, Maria and I have been working through some stuff. We have some ideas but we need to work through further. Yeah, I'll keep you in the loop. What's that? Mark? He's hurting." Jason shot a look behind at Mark and then walked through the house and out the front door. "Okay, I can talk now."

Andrew's voice came through, a sad note in it. "I know he's hurting, Jason. You all are. I wish I knew where she was, Jason, and could sweep in and scoop her up and bring her back. We're working it as best we can, but so far, nothing has come through. It's going cold, Jason, and I don't want that to happen. The officers here and in your town are working as much overtime as they are allowed and even on their own time, trying to find her. Just a sec." Andrew's voice faded for a minute. "Jason, I have to run. Something's come up. Let me know if you find anything."

Jason slowly pocketed his phone, his eyes searching the sky above. Where, Lord, where is she? Am I to lose her too, just like Mom and Dad? Please, I can't do that again. I can't lose my sister. Tears clouded his vision. He turned as he felt a hand on his arm and wrapped his wife in his arms, his tears wetting her hair.

"Jason, has Andrew any word?" She felt him shaking his head. "Come, Mark's found something he's not sure of."

❁ ❁ ❁ ❁

Andrew turned as Bill walked towards him, a folder in his hand. He pointed at his office door. Sinking down in his chair, he sighed.

"What do you have, Bill?"

"Some interesting data on Brown. He's not as lily white as he wants to appear."

Andrew's head shot up and he stared at him. "Mark's investigating his portfolio for him. Does that mean he's involved in all this?"

Bill nodded. "It may well be. He's tried to stay clean in the last five years and if that's what Mark is investigating, he won't find anything. He needs to go back before that, and I would guarantee he hasn't been given that material."

"But I can't see him kidnapping either one of them."

Bill shook his head. "I can't either, but his family? That I can see." He handed the folder to Andrew and sat back. "He has at least one son and two grandsons and a daughter under federal investigation as well. They appear to just skirt the edge of the law and from what I'm finding out, were well over the line into multiple crimes."

Andrew scanned the material, stopping at one point. "I don't like this, Bill. Julia's disappeared and we may not see her again. Who's to say she's even still in the area?"

Bill rose, heading for the door. He closed it, then sat back down. "That's what I'm afraid of, Andrew. I'm afraid she's been taken out of the country. If that's the case, who knows where she is or if she's even safe or alive."

Andrew drew a deep breath. "I don't want to be the one to tell Jason this, or even Mark. What dates are we looking at and how do we get the financial information we need?"

"Already taken care off. Judge Lane signed off on a search warrant and a warrant for financials an hour ago. I have a team heading out to Brown's house now. I'm heading to the bank to serve the warrant there. I'll get what I have to Mark. I worked him in as a consultant on this case. I cleared it with the chief and also Judge Lane."

"You're ahead of me there, Bill. Good work. Glad you're on our side." He rose. "When you get the financials, head out to see Mark. Jason said the three of them were working it as if they were here in the office."

"Mark has a sharp mind. If he couldn't find the information, then it wasn't given to him."

✪ ✪ ✪ ✪

The man stood in the shadowy room, eyes on Julia. She slept in a drug-induced sleep, not moving. He turned to the door, and opening it quietly, looked around. He knew there was only one other person in the house and he wouldn't be moving any time soon. He had taken care of that. Some of the sedative they fed Julia nightly had gone into his meal. He wouldn't be awake for hours.

The man stooped by Julia and gathered her into his arms. Time was running out for her, he knew. He had heard the leader talking. Julia was to disappear the next day, somewhere overseas he suspected, somewhere she would never return from, somewhere her family would never see her again. He couldn't allow that to happen. He crept down the steps, careful to avoid the creaks, and headed for the door. A glance into the living room showed the man who was to be on guard slumped over on the couch, sound asleep.

He walked quietly away from the house, leaving with Julia safe in his arms. He headed for the forest, knowing they would look for him on the roads and streets of the nearby town. He wouldn't go that way. He had been raised in the country and knew the area around here. No one knew him now, he thought. He looked down at Julia's face, showing white against his dark jacket, the moonlight flickering over it as he walked through the forest. Soon, he reached the truck he had stashed there. He set Julia down on her feet, holding her upright as he fished out his keys and unlocked the door, sliding her onto the seat and fastening the seatbelt around her. Shutting the door softly, he stood, looking around, listening. Good, he thought. So far, it looks as if we're safe.

He raised his eyes to the sky. God, we haven't been on talking terms lately, but I really could use Your help. I need to get this young lady to safety and I need You to help me do that. He waited, feeling the peace pass over him. Then he slid behind the wheel and drove away. Took Julia away from the danger she had been in and away from the men who would have taken her away forever from her family and put her into who knew what kind of danger.

Where to now, Lord? I can't take her to her home. They're watching it. Where do I take her? He nodded as he got his answer. Of course! Why hadn't he thought of that? Young Jonah would help.

Chapter 10

Jonah stared at the man standing in front of him. Uncle John? Where had he come from? He hadn't seen him in a couple of years. Now what? His mother had always claimed that John was the black sheep of the family, but Jonah had never seen that. He had seen that his uncle was compassionate, caring, and wanting for justice. Jonah often wondered what he did for a living.

"Jonah, I need your help." John stood just inside the front door, closing it behind him, his cap in his hand. "I have Julia here."

"Julia? How? What?" Jonah reached for the door, but his uncle's hand on his arm stopped him.

"Jonah, wait. We need to make some plans. Let me go get her. Where can she go here?"

Jonah pointed to the guest room. "In there. Why? Is she hurt?"

"I'll explain in a minute. Hold on."

Jonah watched as John returned, cradling Julia in his arms, heading for the guest room. John laid Julia down, brushing her hair back from her face, and ensuring that all was well. He took the quilt Jonah handed him and covered her, before clicking on the lamp at the bedside. He stood for a moment, his eyes on her face, then turned, clicking off the overhead light, leaving the door open.

Jonah pointed to the kitchen, heading there ahead of his uncle, turning to face him once in the room. "Okay, Uncle John. Give. What's the deal?"

"Do you have any coffee, Jonah? I could use some and I know you'll need it by the time I'm through." He pulled out a chair, sinking wearily into it. He was glad this was his last assignment and he could retire. He had had enough.

Jonah set the mug down in front of his uncle, then shooting him a glance, reached for bread and meat, making them both a sandwich.

"Thank you, Jonah. I appreciate this." He sipped his coffee, staring across the room, finally sighing as he set the mug back down, his hands cradling it, drawing warmth into the coldness he felt.

"Tell me, Uncle John. How did you find Julia?"

John held up a finger, pulling out his phone. "I need to send a message, then I'll talk to you. We've needed to have this talk for many years. It involves more than just that young lady in your guest room." Message sent, phone on the table and turned off, John studied his nephew, tracing the family resemblance to his beloved sister. "How's your Mom?"

Jonah stared at him for a moment, then spoke. "She's hurting, Uncle John. She just doesn't understand what happened all those years ago, why you changed."

John shook his head, and reaching into his pocket, pulled out a brown wallet, flipping it open. "This is why. I was approached years ago to help authorities in another county to track and arrest drug runners. I knew the area and they thought I could help. For all these years, Jonah, I have been undercover, working in counties away from here, under an assumed name, just to keep you and your Mom out of the line of fire. That's why. This was my last assignment. I've retired as of today."

Jonah stared at his uncle, finally looking down at the badge lying in front of him. "Mom never knew, did she?"

John shook his head. "No, she never did. I didn't dare tell her what I did. It was much too dangerous. Your Dad knows. I shared it with him when you were younger, so he could watch out for all of you."

Jonah stared at the badge again. "That's why he's like he is, isn't it? He's been on guard for us."

John nodded. "That he has. Now, about Julia. I had to get her out of there tonight and I didn't know where else to take her for the night. I took great risk in this. The man who held her was planning on sending her out of the country tomorrow. And you know what that means. She would never had come home."

Jonah nodded, horror briefly flickering across his face. "So, now what? How do we get her home?"

"Call your friend, Bill is it? Call him out here. I'll have to stay in hiding for now. They'll be after me."

Jonah nodded as he reached for his phone. "Where will you go, Uncle John?"

"Here. I'll just be your uncle come to visit. I don't need to go to town or anywhere like that. If I do, I can disguise myself. In fact, that's what I have been doing, disguising myself, even my voice."

Jonah rose as a knock came at the back door. It would be Bill, he knew, having asked him to come to the back door.

"Bill! Thanks for coming. I don't think you've ever met my uncle, have you?"

Bill stared at the man in front of him, memory struggling to place him. "I don't think I have. Hello." He shook John's hand, then turned to Jonah. "What's so important I had to come out here tonight, Jonah? This is not you."

Jonah handed him a mug of coffee. "We have something we need to speak with you about. First, come with me." Jonah led Bill to the guest room and pointed.

Bill took a look at Jonah, a look into the room, then back at Jonah. Jonah nodded and Bill walked into the room, over to the bed, and stopped, shocked. He stared down at Julia. How, Lord, did she get here? He spun to stare at Jonah, who beckoned him out and back to the kitchen.

"Jonah? How?"

"Uncle John. He brought her here."

Bill spun to stare at John this time, sitting when John pointed at the chair, handing him his badge.

"It's okay, Bill. I've retired as of today, so I can share with you." John explained what had transpired. "Now, you see, this involves much more than just her kidnapping. We need to keep her and her Mark out of harm's way. Now that she's gone, they'll be coming after him again."

Bill nodded, reaching for his phone. "Is it okay if I call Jason?"

"Just warn him that Mark is in grave danger. Say nothing about Julia being here. We need to make plans, and we need to involve your boss."

Bill agreed. "Jason? Bill. Listen, I just got word that Mark's in danger again. We need to put him somewhere safe. They are? That's good. They'll help." He stared at Jonah. "Jason said Zeke and Matthias were there."

"Good. Now what do we do?"

"We need to find somewhere we can keep Julia safe, that they can't track her to. We need to get Mark away as well." Bill stood and paced, finally pulling out his phone. "I need to call Andrew."

"Bill, wait. We need to have some sort of plan in place before we do." John waited until he sat back down. "Where can we put the two of them where they won't be easy to find?"

Bill sighed. "That's the thing. I don't know where. Julia's really well known around town. Mark's getting that way too, given what they've gone through. How do we hide them in Elmton?"

"We don't." Jonah tapped the table with his fingers. "We have to come up with somewhere else."

John looked towards the hallway as he heard a sound from the guest room, then rose and headed that way.

Jonah watched him, then turned to Bill. "Where then, Bill? Where do we put them?"

"Not with any of us, that's for sure. You're in danger just for having her here tonight." Bill turned to look at the doorway, then back at Jonah. "Your uncle cost the man a lot of money tonight."

Jonah frowned as he stared at Bill. "I don't get it, Bill. How?"

"Julia." When Jonah still stared at him, Bill continued, grimness lacing his words, "She wasn't just being sent overseas, Jonah. If it's who we've been looking at, he auctions off the ladies to the highest bidder."

Jonah sat back, a look of horror on his face. "Sells them? That's what would have happened to her?"

Bill nodded, sadness on his face. "I would suspect so. With her beauty, she would have made him millions."

Jonah turned pale and sick at that thought. "God put Uncle John there, didn't

He? To get her away from them. That's why they separated them, isn't it?" He stood, agitation in his movements. "How do we stop this guy?"

Julia stirred, rolling over on the bed to face away from the door, her eyes opening. She listened, her mind still groggy from the drug. She frowned as she stared at the wall. This wasn't the room she had been in, now was it? She heard footsteps approaching and stayed still. When there was no more movement, she turned her head enough to look, drawing in a quick breath as she saw John standing beside her. She pulled herself as far away from him as she could, head down and covered with her arms. She had come to expect a beating whenever one of the men were around her. But not him, she thought, peeking out from under one of her arms.

"You're safe, Julia." He repeated it a couple of times, before she finally raised her head to look at him. "You're safe, Julia. You're at a friend's home. I couldn't let them hurt you."

"You never did." Her voice was hoarse, her throat sore. "Why?"

He shrugged. "It's not who I am. I got you away from them." He pointed at the bed and she nodded. He sat, careful not to get too close to her. "You were to be sent out of the country tomorrow, my dear. I couldn't let them do that to you or your family. I couldn't save any of the other ladies. I didn't know in time. You, I had to."

"Why?"

"Why, what?"

"Why overseas?"

"That's a discussion for another day, my dear. Now, are you thirsty?"

She nodded and hesitating, finally reached for the hand he offered, letting him pull her to her feet. "Where are we?"

"With a friend of Mark's for now. We will have to move to another place, though, to keep you safe."

Bill and Jonah rose to their feet, Jonah trying to cover the horror of what he had just been told, as John appeared in the doorway with Julia, her hand still in his. She stopped, fear in her eyes, as she searched to the faces of the two men in front of her.

"Bill?" Her voice was tentative and low.

"It's me, Julia." A small smile came to his face. "What can we get for you?"

John pulled out a chair for her, but she shook her head, reaching for one the farthest from the men as she could get. The three men shared a glance, sorrow in their eyes. What had happened to her that they didn't know about?

"What can we get you, Julia?" John crouched down beside her, not touching her.

"Tea, if possible. I can't touch water, or juice or coffee. I don't know if I ever will be able to."

He nodded, knowing that's how the man had had the sedatives administered to her, and rose, heading for the kettle. "Do you have tea, Jonah?"

Jonah reached into the cupboard beside him and drew out the tea canister. "Here, let her use Mom's cup and saucer. Maybe that will help."

John nodded. "They always used a mug for her. That will help. Anything that will get her mind from that." He sighed, staring down at the kettle as it started to whistle and then reaching to unplug it. "She'll need some powerful help, Jonah. We need to find that for her. This has broken her in more ways than one."

John set the cup in front of her and caught her attention. "How about some toast, Julia? Would that help?"

She hesitated, then finally nodding. "It might. Whatever they gave me always made me so sick." She looked up at John. "Jason? Is he okay?"

"Jason and Maria are fine, worried about you." He waited for her to ask him the question that hovered on her tongue but knew she wouldn't. "Mark's with Jason. He's fine, Julia, trying his best to find the people responsible for this."

Her eyes flew to his face and he could see a subtle shift in her gaze. *We need Mark here, Lord, but how do we do it?*

"Jonah, can you get Zeke and whoever it was with him to bring Mark out here tomorrow? They're friends of yours, so it won't be off if they do. Jason too. He's always wanted to see your farm, hasn't he?"

Jonah nodded, reaching for his phone, seeing it was after midnight, but knowing Zeke wouldn't care. "We'll get them here. We need to start making plans as well." He stepped to the kitchen door. "I usually don't have lights on this late. I would suggest we shut down some of them. There's a light over the sink I sometimes leave on. Put that on, Uncle John. I'm turning off the lights in the rest of the house, other than in the bathroom. That can stay on. If Mom's here, it's on all night."

Chapter 11

*J*ason stepped down from Zeke's truck, looking around. Jonah has a nice place here, he thought, staring at the one-level sprawling home done in dark-green siding and cream trim with a wide front porch. The barn he could see in the distance matched in colour. He could hear the low moos from the cattle and turned to study the area more fully. Why did they insist I come here today, Lord? Even Andrew pushed.

Mark stopped beside Jason. "It was really rundown when Jonah got it about ten years ago, Jason. He's worked hard to get it where it is. He's trying to switch to organic farming, to do more truck gardening as they call it."

"It's a nice place. If we didn't have the place we did, something like this would suit Maria and I. When Julia marries, the house will be hers."

He turned and followed the three other men to the door, stepping through, and assessing the house and nodding. Not too masculine, he thought. Must be his mother's influence here.

He turned as Jonah approached, greeting his friends, then stopping in front of him, an older man at his side. Jason frowned. He knew the man but couldn't put a name to him.

"Jason. Thanks for coming. This is my Uncle John." He turned to look behind him, uncertainty in his stance. "We have someone I know you're going to be glad to see."

Jason's eyes slid shut. "Julia?" He opened them to see Jonah nod and then compassion filling the eyes of the older man. "Where is she?"

John held up his hand. "She's still sleeping, Jason. Come out to the kitchen. We need to talk and I need to make sure you and Mark are on the same page as we are."

"What do you mean?" Jason's voice was stern and yet held puzzlement.

"Sit. You'll here early enough I know that Zeke didn't let you have breakfast." John turned to him. "Have your wife go somewhere safe today, Jason. It's important she does this and that you talk to her before we tell you what we need to tell you. Andrew's headed this way."

Jason shot him a look, then nodded. Something had happened overnight, and he didn't like the sounds of it. He pocketed his phone. "She's on her way to her Mom's. This was already planned. Andrew's been by and is sending someone with her." He looked between the men as he slid into a chair. "Now, tell me what's up."

"First you eat, Jason. Then we talk and make plans. I want Andrew here when we do. He's about 15 minutes out." Jonah rubbed his hands together, then grasped his mug.

Andrew stood leaning against the counter, listening to the men talk, his eyes flicking between Jason and Mark. They lifted to the hallway as he heard soft footsteps and watched as John rose and headed that way and sighed. He had really wanted to have that conversation they needed to have without Julia there. The men heard quiet conversation between the two they couldn't see. Jason stood and started that way, stopping when Jonah reached a hand out and stopped him, shaking his head at the questioning look.

"Let her come to you, Jason. It's best."

Jason frowned, a puzzled look on his face, then looked at Mark, who also stood watching, heart in his eyes.

John appeared in the doorway, Julia beside him, her hand tight in his. She stopped, eyes widening, fright in her face.

She started to shake her head. "No, Jason, you shouldn't be here." As he took a step towards her, she moved backwards. "It's too dangerous. I can't let them hurt you." Tortured eyes studied her brother, then traveled past him to Mark.

Mark moved to stand beside Jason, his eyes fastened on Julia. "Julia?"

Julie stared at him. "You're safe. They told me they had killed you and buried you somewhere no one would ever find you. They threatened to do the same to Jason and

Maria." Tears filled her eyes as she watched Mark move towards her.

John stepped away, compassion filling his face as he watched Jason wanting to go to his sister yet wanting to honour her request. The men turned, hiding their emotions as Mark stood in front of her, then gathered her close, her arms tightening around him. They could hear her sobs. Then Mark gathered her into his arms and headed for the living room, settling into one of the arms chairs, Julia tight in his grasp. His tears soaked her hair as he held her and let her cry.

Jason spun to stare at Andrew. "Andrew? What's going on?" His hardened gaze took in all the men.

"Sit, Jason. We need to talk. Let Mark deal with Julia for now. Other than John, he's the only male she's allowed to touch her since John brought her here. She's gone out of her way to stay as far away from Jonah and Bill as she can."

Jason sank into a chair. "What aren't you telling me, Andrew?"

Andrew tipped his head to John. "It's his story. He's been under cover for years, Jason. He's the one who got Julia away."

Jason turned to John. "Talk. And leave nothing out." Even as an experienced officer, Jason's face paled as he heard what John had to say. His eyes sought the doorway to the living room and he groaned. "Thank you, John. Did they hurt her?"

"She was beaten, I think, on a daily basis. Other than that, I would say no. I was assigned to guard her and I can say nothing else happened. I couldn't prevent the beatings. They were done while I was away from her. That they did on purpose. The purpose was to break her. That they did. You've seen yourself how scared she is of a man. Except for Mark. He'll be able to reach her."

"But she trusts you." Andrew spoke up.

John nodded. "Not at first. I had to do some talking to get her to trust me."

"So, how does this fit in with what Mark was investigating?" Zeke spoke up, asking the question uppermost in their minds.

"Whoever is in charge wants to know how much Brown has said and if Mark has found the links. Bill's been investigating the men we think are involved, and Mark has been searching further back in the financials. What he was given seems to have been done deliberately to keep him from searching back any further. That's why they wanted what he had been given, to prevent him searching any deeper."

"So now what, Andrew? Where do we put the two of them? We can't leave them separate." Jason faced his superior, questions on his face and in his eyes.

Andrew nodded. "No, we can't leave them apart. We're working on a place, but we need to keep the location to only a few. That means, Jason, that when you leave here, you won't be able to see or contact Julia for a while, not until we have this settled. It's too dangerous for both of you."

Mark looked up as Jason approached and stopped near the chair.

"Mark?"

"She's cried herself to sleep, Jason. I don't want to move and disturb her." Mark tilted his head to look at Julia. "What did they do to her?"

"Beat her every day for one thing. We need to look at her back. John thinks there may be some wounds that need treatment, but he hasn't been able to get her to agree to have them dressed."

Mark nodded, trying to think of how they could do that. "If I hold her up, can you raise her shirt enough to look?"

Jason nodded. "Let's try." He drew in his breath as he saw the deep bruising on her back. "There are no cuts that need dressing, but I think we need to get some photos of her back, for evidence." He turned as Andrew approached, a dark look on his face as he studied Julia.

"Here, Jason. Use my phone. No. Let me take them. That way nothing can be said."

Jason stepped back and watched, Mark cradling Julia back into his arms when Andrew was done. Jason's hand went to his sister's cheek, and his heart broke as she pulled away, burrowing her face deeper into Mark's shoulder. "Will we ever get her to trust again?"

"You will, Jason. It will take time. But first we need to find those men. And we need to find somewhere she'll be safe, as will Mark." Andrew looked up as John approached. "Have you come up with a place yet, John?"

"I think I have. I'll take Mark and Julia with me and leave come dusk. Until then, I would suggest we keep her away from any windows or doors. Jason, by late afternoon, you and the other two will need to be out of here. Bill and Andrew are on their way now."

Jason nodded, sinking into a chair where he could watch Julia. "Will they be safe there, John?"

John shrugged. "I have no idea where they will be safe. Whoever these men are, they've got a good line of intelligence into your town. You need to find that leak and then maybe we can find out who they are."

Jason nodded, his head going back onto the chair. "I know, John. I just wish I could pinpoint who they are. And that's not to say a woman isn't involved."

Mark spoke. "A woman is involved. I can remember hearing a woman's footsteps before they knocked me out and separated us." He frowned. "I had forgotten that. I don't remember her speaking at all though, nor the men talking to her. I got the impression she was up the ranks in leadership though."

Andrew shared a look with Jason, who nodded. "We have some names we're looking into. Now that we know a woman is involved, that will help."

Jason laid his hand on his sister's head and prayed, then turned and walked away, his heart heavy, not knowing when he would see her again, and knowing he couldn't even tell Maria Julia was still alive. He knew she would wonder where Mark ended up. Lord, protect them both, please. Let us bring this to a swift close. I need my sister back in my life. Mark too.

Zeke and Matthias spoke quietly with Jonah, then moved off, leaving John standing watching. John turned and headed back into the house, standing for a moment to watch Mark and Julia. Julia was asleep on the couch, not having roused from earlier that day. Mark sat where he could watch, heart on his face.

"Mark?" John watched as Mark reluctantly turned his eyes from Julia. "We'll be leaving in about an hour. I'm not saying where we're going. It's better if no one knows."

"How do I know I can trust you, John? Sure, you got Julia out and away from those monsters. But I don't know you. How do I trust someone I don't know?"

"That's fair enough, Mark. I can't tell you to trust me. I can only show you. For one thing, that young woman there does. So far, I'm about the only one she's trusting right now. She has to learn to trust all over again. Or didn't you hear what we told you?"

Mark nodded. "I heard. I'm just having a hard time accepting it." He held up his hands. "I know. I know. You're looking out for her and me too. Just let's get going, all right?"

Chapter 12

Mark watched through the windshield as John pulled up to a decrepit-looking house and stopped, leaving the car to put up the garage door. Mark turned to John as he pulled into the garage.

"How long, John, can we stay here?"

John shrugged. "For tonight at least. I have to find somewhere else tomorrow, but we're safe here for now. I was out here earlier and checked it out." He turned to look over his shoulder at Julia. "Julia." He waited until she turned to him. "We're going to get out here and go inside. We don't have to go outside the garage at all. Wait for Mark to help you."

She shook her head. "I can't." Tears shone in her eyes. "I don't know who I can trust anymore, John, other than you."

Mark's heart clenched. What did they do to her to destroy her trust that bad? She was shattered to pieces and he wanted to help mend. Only God could do that, but he wanted to be part of the process.

Julia knew she had hurt Mark with her words, but she just didn't know who she could trust any more. It hurt that her trust had been shattered like that. She moved stiffly, the bruises on her back healing but hurting.

John watched from where he stood, having shut the garage door, and raised his eyes to Mark, his heart going out to the younger man. Patience, Mark, he thought, patience and a lot of prayer. They really did a number on her, he thought. He prayed that they would never have to tell her what the plans for her had been. They just needed to keep her safe and out of the way of those men. Heaven help them if they ever found Julia again. Anyone with her would be dead and she would be gone for good.

Mark paced the kitchen, waiting for John to come back inside. Julia had headed for the bedroom John had assigned her, not speaking a word, not looking at him. He stopped in the kitchen doorway, his eyes on her closed door. When, Lord? When will she trust me again? Is she still trusting You like she did? He turned as John entered, rubbing his hands to get rid of the chill.

"How safe are we really here, John?"

John drew a deep breath. "Safe enough, I think, Mark. Although nowhere is truly safe, not until we catch those guys. What I need is to find somewhere we can hole up and help you go over all that material you've gathered."

"And how do I know I can trust you, that this isn't some big ploy to get Julia back into their hands after you get the information you want?"

"Fair enough, Mark. I'd be asking the same questions if it was me." He moved to make coffee, his back to Mark as he spoke. "Jonah's told me over the years how good you are with financial information. That you won't stop until you've found everything there is to find." He turned, pointing at Mark. "That's going to be your job, finding the information we need to stop these people. I haven't been able to help those other ladies who disappeared. They were gone before I came on the scene. I want to stop this from happening to anyone else if I can."

Mark nodded. "Okay, so what do we do?"

"First, we grab what sleep we can. Julia's down for the night. She's still fighting the two weeks of being heavily drugged at night."

"They drugged her every night?" Mark's face showed his shock.

"They did. They wanted to sleep and they wanted to make sure she didn't get away."

"But how did you get her out of there?"

John shrugged. "All of them left that night except the one man and I. I managed to find the sedative and gave it to him." He paused, a thought crossing his mind. "Julia wasn't as heavily drugged that night." He shook his head, not liking what he was thinking.

"And?"

John looked up at Mark. "And that helped me to get her away and to safety, I think. Never mind. Tell me what you've found."

Mark sighed, knowing John wouldn't tell him what he was thinking, and he wasn't even sure if he wanted to know. "I've found evidence that Brown is highly involved in the rackets, laundering money through various businesses he owns." He accepted the mug of coffee and sat. "I can't sleep, John, not until I find what we're looking for."

John shook his head. "You need to, Mark. We need to both stay as rested as we can. Julia needs that from us. If we don't we'll make mistakes, and those mistakes could get up killed and Julia gone."

Mark stared at John. "I know, John. I know that, but I still want to work some tonight."

John sighed, tired to the bone, but knowing he wouldn't be sleeping if Mark didn't. "All right. Hand over some of that material and I'll see what I can figure out from what you've dug up."

◉ ◉ ◉ ◉

Julia made her way to the kitchen early the next morning, her footsteps cautious and hesitant, her demeanour one of fear. When would she be able to trust fully again, she wondered? She shuddered as she remembered words she had heard when they thought she was unconscious. Please, Lord, keep me safe. Help them to find those men fast so that I can go home. Tears clouded her vision for a minute and she blinked rapidly to clear them. Standing in the doorway, she watched as Mark worked away, not aware she was there. John was nowhere to be seen.

Realizing he wasn't alone, Mark looked up and a smile crossed his face. "Julia. You're awake. What can I get you?"

She shook her head as she moved into the kitchen, keeping a distance between them. "I can get it myself, thank you." A formality had sprung up between them, one that hadn't been there before.

Mark sat back and watched as she worked away at the counter, her movements stiff and jerky. He felt the anger growing in him and prayed for its release. Julia needed his help, not his anger.

"Where's John?"

"He's gone to find another place for us to stay."

She spun, her eyes wide in shock. "He's left? He's not here? I need him here." Panic was setting in.

Mark stood, careful in his movements. "He felt we were safe enough here for a couple of hours. Have your tea, Julia. He said he'd be back soon."

Julia's hands shook as she grasped the mug. Lord, I just can't do this. I look at Mark and I see how he's hurting. He wants to fix it, to make me better and he can't. I'm going to have to walk away from him, from Jason and Maria, from my hometown just to keep them safe, and I know Mark won't let me.

She turned as John came through the door. "Get your stuff. We're out of here now."

"John?" Julia sat, staring at him.

"Now, Julia. What do you have in the bedroom?"

"Just my jacket."

Mark headed that way, checking to see that nothing remained. "They found us, John?"

"It looks that way. We have a bit of time." He studied Julia for a minute. "Julia, do you remember feeling anything like a bug bite or an injection or something like that?"

She stared at him, then nodded, pointing to her left shoulder. "There. It was after one of their sessions. I could barely keep my eyes open, but I remember something."

John nodded. "Let me see the area, please."

She stared at him, then pulled over the neck of her T-shirt. "Right there."

John approached carefully. "I need to touch that area, Julia. I think they implanted a tracking device. If they did, I need to remove it." He felt along the muscle, then sighed. "And they did."

Working quickly, he sterilized his pocket knife, then approached her again. "This will hurt, Julia. I need to make a small cut so I can get the tracker out."

She nodded, then clenched her hands as he cut into the flesh and found the tracking device. "This is how they've found us, I would suspect. Let me bandage you up and we'll be on our way. Now, let me see your jacket. Just as I thought. Did you notice this bulky area?" When she shook her head, he continued, "This is all part of it, Julia. Leave the jacket. I have another I can give you. Now we need to leave."

Mark had stood back, horrified at what John had discovered. "A tracking device? But what?" At John's look, he stopped speaking, then nodded. He knew why without John saying anything.

"There we go, Julia. Now, do you have everything, Mark? You do? Then let's get out of here."

John watched the traffic around him. He had managed to find another car for them to use, but he still felt followed, somehow.

"Mark, Julia. We're heading into Logan City. I'm not telling you what I'm planning or where we're going, but we'll be switching vehicles again."

Julia stared out the window. "Is this all necessary, John?" She sounded resigned to her fate.

Mark and John shot each other a look, knowing that they both were committed to keeping her safe.

"It is, Julia. Mark's getting close to finding what we need. I heard from Andrew. He and Bill are working through the paperwork they've been given. Andrew's brought in another financial investigator as well, Mark, to search out overseas accounts. We'll get them."

"But will we still be alive. John?" Julia's question gave them pause for thought. "I don't imagine the man who had kidnapped will let me live now. I've shamed him and he won't stand for that. I heard him talking about others he's killed."

Chapter 13

Jason looked up from where he was seated in the office as Maria touched his shoulder. He drew her down onto his lap and buried his face in her hair.

"Any word, Jason?" Her question was soft.

"No. Andrew heard from John this morning, but nothing since then. They're on the run. I just pray they are able to stay ahead of the kidnappers." He shuddered as he thought of what Julia had already gone through.

"How close are they to finding them?"

Jason shrugged, his eyes on his wife's face. "I have no idea. Andrew and Bill are keeping things pretty close to only themselves. And I can't say that I blame them. If I was involved, it could compromise the investigation or the evidence chain, and we don't want that." He looked up as the doorbell rang. "Are we expecting anyone at this time of night?"

She shook her head. "Not that I know of."

"Stay here. Be prepared to hit the hiding spot if you need to." He dropped a kiss on her cheek and walked through to the door.

Peeking outside, he opened the door. "Zeke? Jonah? What are you two doing here?" He stood back. "Come in. Maria and I were about to have our dessert and coffee. Come, join us."

Zeke and Jonah shared a glance, then followed Jason to the kitchen. Maria appeared in the doorway and then moved to make fresh coffee.

Seated at the table, dessert and coffee in front of them, Jason reached for Maria's hand. "Now, tell us. What brings you out this way at this time of night?"

Zeke sighed. "I know it's getting late, but Bill asked if we would drop in on you, just as friends." He looked up at Jason, then at Maria. "John got word to Andrew.

They've been followed but he thinks he's managed to get rid of the tracking device."

"Tracking device?" Jason got the look the two men shared again. "Julia."

Maria stared between the three men. "What do you mean, Julia?"

Jason's hand tightened on hers. "With the men like we are chasing down, they will implant tracking devices into their victims. I suspect that's what John meant."

Maria was horrified. "Implanted?"

Jonah nodded. "They do that. Uncle John hasn't said where they're headed, but I know they've been back my way. It's going to take a lot on Uncle John's part to keep them safe. He has a whole network he can draw from, and I think that's what he's going to have to do." He paused as his phone chimed. He stood. "Excuse me. I need to take this."

Maria watched him walk away, then turned back to Zeke. "Zeke, what aren't you two saying?"

"We've said what we've been asked to. We don't have the details that I know you want. It's not safe for us to have them. I would imagine we're all being watched."

Jason nodded. "I can guarantee we are. My worry is for Maria. If they think they can get to Julia through her, they'll try that."

Zeke nodded. "That's what we thought. Andrew has asked us to take her with us tonight. He's arranged for a safe place for her to stay until this is over." He looked over at Maria as she protested. "No, Maria. You need to. If you don't, they'll use you. Where Andrew wants to put you, they won't get near you at all. He's worked with this group before and they're the best at what they do."

Maria shook her head, her eyes on Jason. Jason sighed, pulled her to her feet and away from the room. He finally returned, hands running through his hair.

"She'll go. Who's taking her?"

"The team she'll be staying with will meet us here in about thirty minutes. They'll take her to safety. Jason, you need to be very careful as well. Andrew is very close to putting you under guard as well."

Jason nodded. "I know he is. I can't go."

"That what he said." Jonah looked up at a knock at the door. "That's likely the team now. Is Maria ready?"

Jason nodded as he stood and headed for the door. "She is. Just give me a couple of minutes."

Jason stood, Zeke and Jonah flanking him, as he watched the SUV carrying his wife leave. Please Lord, keep her safe. Help us to end this and bring Julia and Mark back home.

"Now what?" Jason turned to his friends.

"Now, you come with us." Zeke pointed towards his vehicle.

"With you? I didn't know this was part of the plan."

"It is. You're going into hiding too, only not with Maria. Andrew has her safe. He wants you where he can find you quickly and wants you to keep working on the investigation, solely on the investigation."

Jason nodded and turned back to secure his home, not knowing when he would return. "Just let me grab some stuff okay. And I need my briefcase from the office."

John looked up as Julia wandered around the room. Mark sat, paperwork in front of him, a frown in place. John knew he was getting close to where he wanted to be in the investigation. When that happened, John would take the laptop and all the material and get it to Andrew, somehow.

Julia stopped short of the windows, wanting to be out in the open. Her fingers worried the splint on her hand, the bandage almost off the splint. Other fingers hurt from the trauma they had been put through, but she didn't think any had been broken. She turned as she heard John clear his throat.

"Julia, come sit." John patted the seat beside him. When she shook her head, he insisted. "Sit. I need to talk to both you and Mark. Mark, can you leave that for a bit?"

Mark looked up, his thoughts coming back to the room. "I can. I need a break. I've found what I was looking for, John. I have the information Andrew needs. But how to I get it to him?"

"We'll get it to him. But first, I need to talk to you both." John waited until Julia had seated herself, then he looked down at the book on his knee. "I've been reading through the Bible, you two, looking for answers and guidance." He looked up, a faraway look in his eyes. "I never had the chance to have what you two have for long. I was in love with a wonderful lady, but she didn't live past 25. We only had a few short years together before she went home. I want more than that for you two." His eyes studied first Mark, then Julia, noting how Mark watched Julia, heart in his eyes. Julia, on the other hand, had her eyes fixed on him.

John sighed, seeing the loss of innocence and the pain in her eyes. He hated that had happened to her. Somehow, Lord, give me the words I need to start her healing. Reach down and touch her, please.

He cited his Bible. "You both know that this Book is filled with verses for victory, for trust, for protection, for healing. Whatever we go through in the next few days, remember that God is your strong tower. Run to Him. He has you in the hollow of His hand and covered with His wings. He also provides healing." He turned to Julia. "You're familiar with the passage of the woman who touched His robe. What kind of healing did she experience?"

Julia frowned, her eyes narrowing. "Physical."

He nodded. "But He provided more than that to her. He provided spiritual healing, physical healing, emotional healing, mental healing, psychological healing. All that and more. Julia, please, think and meditate on those verses. They are what you need. You need healing and only God can provide that for you."

He turned to Mark. "I know you're hurting as well, Mark. The lady you love has been hurt and you want to make it all better for her. You can't. You need to walk beside her, providing your strength and the protection she needs. I have no idea when this will be all over or what we'll face, whether we'll still be together or if we'll have to split up again. Julia, we have Jason and Maria safe. Andrew looked after that."

Julia drew a breath of relief. "Thank you, John. I was worried that someone would get to them. Now what?"

"Mark, how long will it take you to finish off what you're working on?"

"An hour, tops. I'll change the password on the laptop so Andrew or Bill can access it and include all the paperwork I have." He looked up again at John. "But how do we get it to them?"

"You leave that to me. Now, Julia, we need to do something about your hair."

"I refuse to cut it." She stood and went to walk away, but John caught her arm.

"No more of that, Julia. You can't walk away from me, ever. Get that?" He stared at her until she nodded. "It could mean your life, Mark's life, or the life of Jason or Maria. Do you understand?"

Frightened, she nodded, her eyes going from John to Mark. "But what do we do, John?"

"Stay here." He left the room and was back in minutes. He handed a pack to Mark and one to Julia. "We're changing our appearance. No more neat and tidy for us. That's a giveaway. Julia, you need to change how you look and I mean really change how you look. In the pack is makeup you would never wear. You'll put it on. There's a man's hat in there as well. Pin your hair up and tuck it up under the hat."

She stared at him, then opened the pack. "Really, John. Goth?"

He nodded. "It's the complete opposite of how you look. There are also contact lenses in there to change your eye colour. Your eyes are too unique. Mark, you'll find clothing in there that aren't what you would usually wear. Don't shave. We're going for the grunge look, you and I."

Mark nodded, his eyes on Julia. "Julia, John knows what he's doing. He's worked undercover for too many years for us not to trust him."

She finally nodded. "How long do we have?"

"As soon as Mark's finished with his paperwork and changed, we need to leave."

John watched as she walked away, then turned as Mark spoke.

"Will this work, John?"

John shrugged. "So far, they've been able to track us. We need to leave everything but what we have on in this place. When you're done with your laptop power it down and stuff it into this knapsack with your paperwork. We'll get it to Andrew or Bill before we move on to somewhere else."

Mark turned his eyes to where Julia had disappeared. "We need to end this sooner than later, John. The longer it takes, the more at risk she is."

John nodded, already knowing that. "I know, Mark. I know. Andrew has been in touch. I've gotten work to him that we'll be moving constantly. It's going to wearing and tiring but we need to do that."

Chapter 14

Andrew looked up as Bill knocked on his office door and he beckoned him in, pointing at the door.

Bill closed it behind him and sat, a knapsack in his hands.

"John came through. This is what Mark had been working on. John came through last night and left it on my porch."

"He did? I'm surprised he took a chance like that."

Bill started to laugh. "If you had seen him, you wouldn't say that."

Andrew shot him a look, then smiled. "Up to his old tricks?"

Bill nodded. "He is, for all of them." He looked down at the knapsack. "I understand Mark has found the information we needed. It's on his laptop and also on paper."

"His laptop? And it's password protected, I suppose?"

"It is, but I'm told he changed it to something we can figure out without his help." Bill pulled out the laptop and powered it up. "Now to try and think like Mark."

"Please, don't. We only need one of him."

Bill laughed at Andrew's joke, then stared at the screen. "What would he use?"

"Try Julia or her last name."

"You think?" Typing in Julia, he watched the screen flicker and then open to the desktop. "We're in. Okay, so now what?"

Andrew came around the desk and stood behind Bill. "He'll have saved it in such a way that no one other than an investigator would find it." He stared at the screen, then with a few quiet words to Bill, the folders opened up.

Andrew studied them, his heart sinking as he read through them. It was much deeper and wider than even he had expected. "Mark's good, Bill."

"That he is. But what do we do with this? We'll need a team to investigate. There's too much for us to do so in a short enough period of time to keep them safe. They can't stay on the run forever."

Andrew nodded, his eyes staring at the wall of his office, not seeing the awards hanging there. "We need to pull in someone. Get in touch with that firm we use as consultants and ask them to help you work through this."

Bill nodded. "I will."

❂ ❂ ❂ ❂

Mark turned to face Julia as she spoke, her words quiet.

"Mark, I need you to go home. It's too dangerous for you. Please."

"It won't work, Julia." He closed the distance between her, even knowing she was withdrawing from him. "It just won't work. They know we're together. If I leave, they'll come after me to get to you. It's better if we stay together."

She sighed, wrapping her arms around herself. "I know, Mark. I just don't want anyone else hurt."

He reached a finger to touch her cheek, watching her reaction. She was uncomfortable, he could tell, but she didn't move away from him. "I'm not leaving you again, Julia. Never again. We fight this through together. There may come a time we'll need to split up, but I stay with you at all times. Do you get that?"

She nodded, fear sparking in her eyes for a moment. "I do, Mark. I really do get that, but I don't have to like it." She turned to pace away, finding John standing behind her. She jumped, not having heard him approach. "John! When did you get back?"

"Just now." He shared a look with Mark, then looked past him at the building they were standing outside of. "This isn't a good spot to be having that discussion, you two. Now, come. I've gotten a new vehicle but I'm not sure how long it will be before they find us again."

"How are they doing that, John?" Mark questioned him as he shut the door behind him, Julia in the centre seat of the truck.

"I don't know, Mark. I've been very careful who I've talked to, where I've been.

We found that tracker and got rid of it. Your laptop is nowhere around." He tapped the steering wheel, then turned the key in the ignition. "We need to get away from here. And I have no idea where to take you two to keep you safe."

John studied the roads around him, trying to determine which route to take, finally heading off towards Logan City.

"Why this way, John?" Julia was puzzled at his move.

"I'm trying to come up with a place for tonight. They'll be looking at the homeless shelters for sure, bus stations, the airport."

Mark turned from the window. "What about an abandoned building?"

John nodded. "We can try that, but I suspect they've already searched them all and will be back through them. I need to stash the truck somewhere too, until tomorrow." He sighed. "And we need to get something to eat. Mark, here's a fast food place. Take this and go get us something. It's not the best food to eat but we need to have something."

John watched as Mark headed back towards them, paper sacks in hand. He hadn't seen anyone watching them but he knew they weren't safe and wouldn't be until they found the culprits and had them in jail.

"Thanks, Mark. Now we eat and then we move."

"Should we be staying here?" Julia asked.

"We can while we eat. Then we move out." He pulled out a phone. "Don't worry, they can't trace this one. Good, Andrew has your information, Mark, and he's pulled in an independent consultant."

Mark nodded, his thoughts racing ahead to the morrow. "I don't like this, John. Where are we going? Have you come up with a place?"

Julia's eyes bobbed between the two men as she nibbled at the hamburger Mark had picked up of her, finally stuffing it back into the bag.

"You need to eat, Julia." John watched as she shook her head.

"I can't, John. I have no appetite. I usually don't eat fast food anyway."

"Eat, Julia, whether you want to or not. I can't guarantee when you'll next have a meal."

She shot him a startled look, then pulled the hamburger back out, eyeing it distastefully. "Do I really have to eat this?"

"Eat it when it's still warm. It's not so nice when it's cold." Mark shared a look with John, then shook his head. "Eat, Julia, and stop this nonsense. John's trying his best to keep us both alive. Or at least doing his best to keep you from disappearing."

"What do you mean?" Her tone was belligerent as she turned to him.

"What do you think was going to happen to you, Julia? Did you really think they would let you go?" Mark was angry and his words had a bite to them, one she had never heard before and she jumped. "Don't you get it? John pulled you out of that house just in time. They were planning on taking you to an airport, putting you on a private jet, and flying you outside of the country, likely overseas, early the next morning. Do you really not understand what

156

that mean?" He turned to her, noting her shocked look. "Don't you get it? Female? Auction? Highest bidder? Never seen again?"

Her hand was at her mouth as his words sunk it and horror flooded her face. The tears she had been holding back started to flow. John shook his head at Mark, wishing he hadn't said anything.

Mark sighed, took the food back from her hands and pulled her close. "Don't you see, Julia? I don't want to lose you. You're too important to me and I thought I was getting to be that for you." His arms tightened around her. "That's why you were beaten every day, to break you so you would never fight back, ever. And they succeeded in breaking you. I can see you've shattered. You'll never be the same, your dreams will never be the same, but let God pick up the shards and put them back together. He'll make something beautiful again. Just trust Him. Just trust us."

He felt her relax against him. He didn't think that would have happened so quickly. He looked down. "She's asleep, John.

"Figured she would be. Don't know if you should have told her, at least not in that manner."

"She wouldn't listen to it any other way. That much I've learned about her. She needs the information fast and in her face."

John nodded as he pulled out of the parking lot. "Now you've told her, you'd better stick around to pick up the pieces."

"I intend to, God willing. She's too important to me, John, to do otherwise."

John pulled into the laneway of an abandoned looking house. "We'll stay here tonight."

"Here?"

John stopped in front of a barn and left the vehicle long enough to open the doors to pull in. " For tonight. I don't think anyone knows of this place, at least not yet. If we have to, we can leave the back way."

Chapter 15

*J*ulia stirred early the next morning, pulling the blanket up higher against the chilly air. She lay there, cuddling down into the straw, eyes closed, her thoughts on Mark. Why won't he leave me, Lord? I don't want him around me. I don't want him hurt because of me. She opened her eyes and glanced around. Where were they? Rolling over, she searched for John or Mark, seeing neither one. She was on her feet, heading for the door she could see, when Mark appeared from behind the truck.

"Julia?"

She spun, hand to her throat. "Mark! You scared me. I didn't see either you or John."

"John's outside, making sure we weren't followed. We were letting you sleep, but now you're away, we'll need to get moving again." He brushed past her to gather the blanket she had been using, but stopped when her hand touched his arm.

"Thank you, Mark, for what you're doing. I know.." Her words broke off as John ran through the door.

"We need to move now, people. Out the back door and towards the woods. Mark, catch." John tossed him a backpack and slipped a second one over his shoulders. "What are you waiting for? Move!"

Mark grabbed Julia's hand and ran for the back door, heading towards the trees he could see. He heard John's pounding footsteps behind him. Once in the trees, John slipped ahead of him, motioning for them to be silent. Mark pulled Julia with him, their pace rapid as they sought to put space and time between themselves and the barn. Finally, John slid to a stop, breathing heavy and looking behind him.

Julia opened her mouth to speak, but shut it abruptly at John's glare. He shook his head, finger to his lips. Then, he pointed to their right, to a little used game trail.

"Mark, led us. This takes us out to the old quarry. From there, I'll take over."

Mark nodded and once more gripped Julia's hand tight in his as they moved forward as rapidly as they could.

Finally, John stopped them, leaning over to brace his hands on his knees, gulping in air.

"John?" Mark's quiet question hung in the air.

"Somehow they spotted us and I have no idea how they did that. No one know about this place." He studied their footwear. "Julia, your shoes. Let me see them."

She stared at him, then down at her feet, not moving.

"Julia, your shoes. Let me see them."

When she still didn't move, Mark reached and pulled her shoes off, handing one to John as he searched the other one.

"Here we go. They placed a tracker in her shoes as well. You have no jewelry on do you, Julia?"

She nodded, lifting a necklace from under her shirt. John reached for it, feeling it. "Another one. Let's hope these are all there are. You're sure you didn't feel any stings anywhere than on your shoulder?"

She shook her head. "Not that I remember, but if it was when I was unconscious, I would never know."

"We'll have to chance that. Now, let's move. They'll be following these. Mark, let me lead." John stopped, staring at Mark. "Have you ever handled a weapon before?"

Mark shook his head. "Never. I've had no reason to."

John nodded. "You may at some point. Be prepared if I hand you one."

Julia spoke up. "I've had weapon training. I had planned on going into the police force like Jason and had gone through the academy, then changed my mind. I can handle a weapon."

Mark stared at her. "You never told me that."

She shook her head. "It's not something I'm proud to have done. Let it rest, Mark."

John finally halted at the bottom of the quarry and looked around. He knew there was another way out of it that not too many people were aware of. But first, he had to make sure they were followed.

"There's a cave over there. You two tuck yourselves in it. If for some reason I don't get back, follow the wall for about 500 yards. You'll find a small opening behind a bent birch tree. It looks as if it's too small to get into but you can manage it. I can. Follow it. It will take you out to the other side of the quarry. From there, head for the trees. You'll find another cave up on that trail. Tuck yourselves into it if you have to. I'll find you." He searched their faces, then turned to Julia. "Here's my extra weapon. You'll find extra ammo in this backpack." He handed her his backpack. "Now go. If you get lost, look for the crooked pine tree at the top of the quarry wall. It will lead you to the other side of the forest if you walk away from it." John was gone before they could say anything.

Mark leaned back against the cave wall, Julia tucked to his side, breathing hard. He had never been through something like this, and he hoped he never had to again. He worked with numbers and turned his results over to the authorities. He wasn't the one who had to be on the run.

Julia touched his arm and pointed at his watch. He nodded. John had been gone

163

for thirty minutes. He peeked out and not seeing anyone, grasped Julia's hand and pulled her behind him along the wall. Finding the tree just where John said it would be, he ducked behind it

"We'll never fit in there." Julia's whisper stirred the hair around his ear.

He shook his head. "John said he can fit into it, so we should be able to. Come on." He slipped into the opening, finding it widened just inside. He walked forward at a rapid pace, hearing Julia's step right behind him and knowing her hand rested on his backpack. At the end of the trail, he stopped.

"Why are we stopping?"

"Ssh! I want to make sure we're alone."

Finally, Mark made a movement to walk forward, reaching back for Julia's hand. She hesitated, then grasped his. She had to learn to trust again at some point, didn't she, she thought? It might as well be with Mark. Jason certainly wasn't there for that to happen with.

The quarry walls raised high above them, and Mark scanned the top as best he could. He had no idea what he was looking for other than someone staring down at them and that likely wasn't going to happen.

"Mark, where did John say the cave was?"

"I can't remember. Can you?"

She shook her head. "I can remember him telling us to look for the crooked pine tree and walk away from it. Is that what we're doing?"

Mark gave a low laugh. "I have no idea. I've never been a fugitive on the run before, so I don't know what we're looking for or where we're heading."

She shook her head again. "Neither do I. Let's hope John catches up with us soon."

He turned as he heard a sound, then pulling her with him, ran once more for the trees, searching for an area they could hide in. He found what he wanted, parting the brush and shoving her through, pulling the brush back into place behind him. He pointed at the tangle of roots.

"In there," he whispered. "We should be able to hide in there."

"Mark, our footprints."

"Let's hope they're not that observant and they're tracking by sight only, not tracking our footprints. Now, ssh!"

Mark and Julia scooted into the opening of the large root ball and crouched down as low as they could get. Listening intently, they heard the running footsteps passing them by and then coming back their way.

"Where are they? They had to come this way."

Julia covered her mouth to keep her gasp quiet. It was one of her kidnappers, she was sure. She buried her head against Mark's back, then clutched the weapon tighter in her hands. They listened to the discussion, finally hearing the men move away.

Julia went to speak, but Mark stopped her with a finger to her lips and a shake of his head. He sat back, head leaning on the roots as he caught his breath. Julia slumped beside her, her hand still gripping the weapon.

Finally, Mark turned to her and smiled. She gave a tentative smile back, before her eyes slid past him to the brush where they had entered.

"Now what, Mark?"

"I have no idea, Julia. I don't know if John is out there still or if they took him out. We'll need to act as if he was." He pointed at the weapon. "Tell me, would you really have used that?"

She raised her hand, staring at the weapon. "I have no idea. Maybe. I don't know."

He started to laugh, keeping it low. "Well, that's very definite. Come on, let's see how we can get out of here without going back onto that path. There has to be another way out."

She nodded, then stared past him once more. "Is this one of those times God covered us with His hands, to hide us?"

Mark studied her, then looked around at the root ball they had taken refuge in. "I would say it is, Julia. It will be something to tell our kids one day."

She sat back, staring at him. "Our kids? What are you talking about?"

He smiled, the smile gentle this time, as he reached to cup her cheek. "Our kids, Julia. You're not getting away from me, not ever. That's just a fair warning that when we get out of this and are safe, I want to pursue what is happening between us. And don't deny it, please."

Her eyes softened and she finally nodded. "We'll see, Mark." She looked at her hands, then raised them to her eyes. "I need to get rid of these contacts. I can't wear them any more."

He nodded, then finally rose to his feet, dragging his backpack with him and made his way out of the root ball, reaching back to help her. He looked around, then headed down the hill, away from the tree, without going back onto the path. There was an animal trail going down that way. Please, Lord, let it lead us to safety. I can't handle it if she's in trouble much longer.

Julia watched as Mark strode ahead of her, tall, strong, confident even in a situation he had never been in before.   Her heart breaking inside her, she kept her cries soft, not wanting him to hear and stop to comfort her. Lord, I need healing. I need to put this behind, to put behind me what those men had planned.   She shuddered at she remembered Mark's words. Please, Lord, get us to safety once more. Tuck us somewhere safe, under the shadow of Your wings. She snuck a peek behind her, at the roots that had protected them. How long had that been prepared for us, Lord? You knew when it went down, didn't You, Lord, that we would need that protection?

Chapter 16

*A*ndrew looked up as Bill approached him in the break room, then pointed towards the board room where their team was working their way through the myriad documents and pieces of information.

"You look troubled, Bill. What's up?"

Bill shook his head. "Someone just brought John into the hospital. He's been shot. The doctors think within the last twelve hours. No sign of either Mark or Julia."

Andrew stopped suddenly enough that the coffee in his mug sloshed close to the rim. "John? That's not good. Can we talk to him?"

Bill turned to look around him, then spoke quietly. "No. The doctors aren't even sure if he'll make it. From what the patrol officers have said, he was near the old quarry and was ambushed. They've followed footprints leading away from him.

We can only surmise that they separated and he went one way to try and lead them away from Mark and Julia."

Andrew nodded. "Okay. So we now have no idea where those two are. Tell you what, get Tad and his wife. Send them out with their dog and see if they can pick up a scent somewhere and follow it. They may be our only hope to find them. I don't want to send out a complete search team. That would be too obvious. Tad and his wife should be sufficient."

Bill agreed and headed for the phone, stopping when Andrew spoke again. "We have someone with John?"

Bill turned. "We do. I've brought in another security team to help. Our guys are getting mad, Andrew. They want whoever this is."

Andrew nodded. "I know. So do I."

❂ ❂ ❂ ❂

Jonah turned from his uncle's bed and found the couch, stretching out. It had been a long day since he had gotten the call that his uncle had been found and brought in to the hospital in critical condition. He glanced at the door, glad there was someone standing

171

guard out there. He sighed. Tomorrow, he would have to go back to his farm. He had produce he needed to harvest.

A sound at the door had him on his feet and he watched as it opened, breathing a sigh of relief when he saw friends there.

Zeke walked in, followed by Josiah. "How is he?"

"Still critical. It's still touch and go, Zeke. Josiah, what are you two doing here?"

"To support you, of course." Josiah gave a quick grin. "Now, tell us what you need done tomorrow on your farm. We're all heading out that way, as are some of the neighbouring farmers. We'll take care of your place until you feel you can leave John."

Jonah stared at them, then nodded. "Okay. I'll give you a list. Any word on Mark and Julia?"

Zeke and Josiah shared a look, then shook their heads. "It's like they've disappeared into thin air. Bill is sending out a search team, but he's not really expecting to find anything."

Jonah nodded. "I pray they do. We need those two back and safe."

❁ ❁ ❁ ❁

Mark stirred, the sounds of the early morning forest awakening him. He rubbed his face, his eyes searching around them. *How long, Lord, do we need to run, to be out here?* He sighed, knowing he was really tired and that was affecting his prayers. He rose, standing watching Julia sleep, knowing he would need to awaken her. Glancing at his watch, he saw it was really early.

"Julia. Come on, sweetheart. We need to get moving." Mark crouched beside her, not touching her.

Julia stirred, her eyes opening, a smile on her face for Mark. "What time is it?"

"It's early. We need to get moving. I hope we can find somewhere we can get some food."

She nodded, reaching into her backpack and pulling out bottles of water. "Here. John has some granola bars as well. We'll eat, then move out." She looked around, shuddering. "Did we lose them, Mark?"

173

"I pray we did, but we can't be sure. We need to get somewhere safe, sweetheart, and hopefully we can do that today."

He reached and helped her to her feet, handing her the lighter of the two backpacks. His leg was aching but he ignored it, wanting to put room between them and the men pursuing them.

"Are they out here, Mark?"

He shrugged. "Not likely, not at this time of day."

He paused a couple of hours later, watching as Julia sank to the ground. She can't take much more, he thought. I need to find somewhere we'll be safe, and I have no idea where. He spun as he heard a sound behind him, his heart sinking. No, Lord. Please, no. Not the men.

A man and woman stepped into view, a Border collie alert and watchful in front of them. Mark watched as they hesitated, then walked towards them.

"Mark Benson?" The man spoke, eyeing Julia as she jumped to her feet and stood behind Mark, her hand going to her pocket. "I'm Tad, with the police. This is my wife, Suzie. We're here to get you to safety."

"Don't take this the wrong way, but can I see some sort of identification?" Mark refused to back down, keeping Julia tucked behind him.

"Sure." Tad pulled out his wallet and handed it to Mark.

Mark eyed him, then opened the wallet. "It's okay, Julia. He's who he says he is." He felt her relax behind him, her hand opening and the weapon dropping.

Tad studied them, then looked at the ground. "I'll take that, Miss Sawyer. You'll not need it. Now, where were you two heading?"

Mark shrugged. "We were trying to find somewhere we'd be safe."

Tad and his wife exchanged a glance. "Fair enough. Now, let's move, okay? We passed the men looking for you during the night, but I'm sure they'll be up and trying to find you soon. Head that way." Tad pointed to their left. "That will take us to where we can get a ride back to our vehicle."

Mark caught Julia's hand in his and felt her grip his with as much strength as she could. He knew she was still uncertain of what she was facing, of the couple walking with them. Suzie was in the lead, Tad behind them. Mark could sense their uneasiness and prayed they made it to safety soon.

Suzie stopped, waiting for Tad to come around the couple to her. They were at the edge of the forest and she could see a vehicle sitting there.

"Is that the one, Tad, that Bill said he'd leave here?"

Tad nodded, looking around. "Stay here, as hidden as you can get, while I go check it out." He shot a glance behind him at Mark and Julia. "They can't take much more, can they?"

She shook her head. "No, they can't. Do you knew where to take them?"

Tad nodded. "Bill and Andrew have come up with a plan and told me where to hide them."

Mark watched as Tad headed for the vehicle and then disappeared on the other side.   Julie clung to his hand, her body behind him as much as she could get. That she was uncomfortable was an understatement, he thought.   His head turned, he watched behind them, worried that they wouldn't make it away before the men came. He turned as he heard footsteps and saw Suzie moving towards Tad, then turning towards them.   She nodded and headed for the truck, as Tad came in their direction.

"Okay. It will be a tight squeeze, but we don't have that far to go. Let's get you two out of here and to a safe location."

The three headed for the truck, Suzie behind the wheel. Tad scooped up the dog as Julia and then Mark squeezed onto the seat, Tad following.   Tad shut the door behind him, the dog on his knee, looking back around where they had come from.

"Ok, Suzie. Let's go."

She nodded and drove off, the dust settling behind the vehicle. The three men who ran for the opening in the forest were too late. Frustration showed in their actions as one threw the branch he had been carrying and loud angry words drove the birds to quiet.

Tad glanced over at Julia, noted the fear on her face. "Mark, just so you know, Andrew's called me. He has a place for you to go to, but we're holding off until later today. He wants to make sure you two haven't picked up anyone else. Suzie's heading for our vehicle. She'll take her dog and head out. Then the three of us will follow."

Mark nodded, watching Julia's face as he did so. Lord, she's so scared. Please bring a resolution to this and quickly. I don't think she can take more.

"Where are we headed then?" He turned his head to look at Tad, meeting their dog nose to nose. A stare and then the dog's tongue came out and swiped across his face.

"Beauty, you really didn't have to do that, you know?" Suzie commented to the dog, a laugh in her voice. "We should have warned you." She watched as the dog scrambled off Tad's knee and laid across both Mark's & Julia's. "Beauty, behave now."

Tad grinned at his wife, then looked at Julia. "First, we're heading for our place. It's safe for now. It will let you two get cleaned up and get some sleep that's not out in the open. A couple of good meals and then we'll talk about where you'll be heading."

"Are you sure we'll be safe?" Julia's voice was barely audible.

"You will be, Julia." Tad promised. "No one should know where you are or who you're with."

Beauty scrambled back on Tad's knee and then leapt from the truck when he opened the door, barely waiting until Mark and Julia were out before jumping back in, settling in Tad's seat. Suzie waved as she drove away.

"All right, into the vehicle with you." Tad searched the area, confident they were alone. "Let's get you out of here."

Julia stopped inside the front door to Tad's home, looking around, feeling very uncomfortable at being there. Mark watched her face, his heart breaking at the uncertainty and lack of confidence in her now. *Lord, we need to get that back for her.*

But how do we do that?   I'm open to any ideas You might want to send my way.

Suzie appeared at the top of the stairs. "This way.   Julia, I've put some clothes in this room for you.   There's an attached bath. Take all the time you want.   Mark, across here.   You and Tad are about the same size. I've left some clothes for you as well. Again, it has its own bath.   The bonuses of having a large home.   Come down when you're ready."   She walked away and down the stairs, looking for Tad.

Tad turned from the back door and just opened his arms for Suzie to walk into them. He felt her tears start and hugged her close.

"It's so sad, Tad.   What can we do to help them?"

Tad sighed.   "Prayer, Suzie.   They need lots of prayer.   Andrew told me what was going on with Julia.   It's not pretty at all. I wish she'd let you check out her back. Andrew said she's been beaten.   But her trust level isn't there.   She's not even truly trusting Mark.   Let's get them fed and let them sleep for a while."   He leaned back to look down at her face.   "I need to head over to find Andrew or Bill. Then I'll be back. Lock up tight and set the alarm."

Suzie watched him walk away, then turned to the kitchen. What could she give them that would be easy for them to eat and yet fill them up? She reached into the freezer and pulled out soup.

Chapter 17

$\mathcal{J}$ulia crept down the stairs, cautious in her movements. Mark seemed to trust this couple, but she just wasn't sure any more who she could or couldn't trust. Even Mark she wasn't too sure about any more. She sighed. Lord, help me.

Mark appeared in the hallway, an easy smile on his face. "Julia. I was just coming to find you to see if you wanted anything to eat." He held out his hand, no pressure on her to take it.

She studied it, then turned to study Mark's face. She could see something there, something she couldn't quite read. Finally, she sighed and took his hand.

"I'm sorry, Mark. I just don't know any more."

Mark nodded, watching her face. "I know, sweetheart. I know. God's got you. Now, Suzie has some soup ready for us, and

I must say, it smells delicious. Come, let's get some food into us, and then I think you'll be wanting to lie down." He stopped. "How's the back?"

"It hurts. How would you think it would feel?"

He grinned at her response, then sobered. "Suzie's a physician. If you feel you need her to take a look at your back, she will. No pressure for that either."

She nodded, then brushed past him, dropping his hand as she did so. "You said there was food. Let's eat."

◉ ◉ ◉ ◉

Tad was on a search. He hadn't found Andrew at the department, nor Bill either. He finally tracked them down at a local diner. He slid onto the seat beside Bill and waved at the waitress as she held up the coffee pot.

"You have news, Tad?" Andrew's voice was quiet.

"I do. They're safe for now."

Andrew relaxed. "Did you see their tail?"

Tad shook his head. "No, but that doesn't mean they weren't there. Mark said they hid on them sometime last yesterday. In a fallen tree root ball of all things."

Bill choked on his food. "Really? That would have been cool to see."

"Bill!" Andrew shook his head at him, then waited as Tad gave his order. "Now what?"

"Now we place them somewhere. I know you had an idea. I have a couple of my own."

Andrew nodded, his eyes watchful. "Have they said much?"

Tad shook his head. "Not yet. Julia has real trust issues right now." He stared at Andrew. "You haven't seen or talked to her, I take it, since at Jonah's?" When Andrew shook his head, Tad sighed. "It's bad, Andrew. I take it that John was able to let you know some of what's going on? When we're done, let's walk and I'll fill you in."

The three men headed for a quieter section of the downtown, their eyes watchful.

"Okay, Tad.   Fill us in." Andrew stopped, his hands in his jacket pocket.

"Like I said, it's bad.   Julia doesn't trust anyone any more, not even really Mark. Mark said she was beaten on a daily basis, and that she has wounds on her back she won't let anyone near to treat.   I'm praying Suzie will be able to reach her and do just that." He looked into the distance. "She's fragile right now, guys. I don't think she can take much more."

"I don't expect she can." Bill turned in a circle, watchful. "Someone's watching us, fellows. Tad, you'll need to be careful going home. If they even suspect you have them, they'll be after you."

Andrew agreed. "Now where do we stash them?"

Tad had come up with a plan. Bill and Andrew stared at him, then stared to laugh.

"That's perfect!"   Andrew agreed. "Will he go for it?"

"I'm sure he will. I've already talked to him. We'll head out that way tomorrow. We just have to get through tonight."

Andrew pulled out his phone that was chiming incessantly. "Well, well. Brown is in custody. The town guys came through." He looked up at the two men. "We have him for what Mark was looking into, the money laundering. But somehow I don't think we're through with whoever it is after Julia."

Bill shook his head. "Brown doesn't have the smarts or the connections for that. Who else would be after her?"

Tad watched and listened at the two men bounced ideas between them, then finally spoke. His words and questions stopped them. They stared at each other, new problems cropping up they could see.

"Well, that does change it all, doesn't it?" Andrew was dumbfounded. "How did we miss that?"

Tad shrugged. "It happens to us all. Now, I'm off to my office. Keep in touch."

"We will. Tad?" Andrew waited until Tad turned back to him. "Be very careful. Whoever it is will stop at nothing, including murder."

"I know. How's John?"

"Still critical. Josiah was by last night. Jonah told him they weren't even sure yet if John would survive."

Tad nodded, a tight look on his face. "Catch you later."

Bill and Andrew stared at one another before heading back to the department. "What did we miss, Andrew?"

"That's what I want to find out. One of us will need to talk to Jason, to find out if there is anything else in her past."

Bill stopped abruptly, eyes sliding closed. "There is, Andrew. How did I ever forget it?" As Andrew watched him, he spoke.

Andrew nodded. "That would be all it would take, now wouldn't it? Let's get back and start digging. Pull in whoever you need, Bill. We need this finished yesterday."

❂ ❂ ❂ ❂

As Tad shut the door behind him, a piercing scream rang through the house. He heard a thump upstairs and ran for the stairs, Suzie right behind him.

"Julia?" Mark was banging at Julia's door. "Julia?"

187

When she didn't respond, he threw the door open, frantic in his search for the woman who had his heart. Tad and Suzie were behind him.

"Oh, Julia!" Mark finally found her cowering in the corner, as small as she could make herself, hands and arms covering her head.

Their hearts broke as they listened to her sobs and pleas not to be hurt, not to be struck again. Suzie buried her head against her husband as he held her. Mark slid to the floor, two feet from Julia, and just watched. He finally laid his hand out, palm up, and let it rest near her. Quiet words didn't help. He finally started to hum and quietly sing some of the old hymns and newer worship choruses he loved.

Tad watched as Julia gradually relaxed, the sobs softening. Julia finally raised her head a bit and lowered her arms, her eyes fastened on Mark. She didn't make a move towards him, just watched. Mark kept his eyes focused on the wall opposite him, his hand still outstretched. He heard Tad and Suzie step back from the room and knew they hadn't gone far.

Finally, Julia's hand came out in a tentative manner and touched his. After a time, her fingers clutched his hand. At that, he turned to look at her, heart sore at the torture in her eyes.

"Come here, sweetheart." He tugged her hand gently. After a few minutes, she moved towards him, uncertainty in her demeanour. Mark pulled her to him, cradling her close, head resting on her hair. He didn't dare move, didn't dare rise.

Julia finally felt safe that day. Mark's arms holding her helped. Her head on his shoulder, her eyes closed and her breathing evened out as she slept. Mark just sat, holding her close, not sure what he should be doing.

Tad appeared back in the doorway and then approached.

"She's sleeping?" At Mark's nod, he quietly continued, "What just happened, Mark?"

Mark finally raised his eyes to Tad. "She was reliving the beatings, Tad. They beat her every single day. Look what they've done to her." Mark had to tamp down his anger. "Why? Why did they have to go and do that? Have you found the ones responsible yet?"

Tad sat down on the bed, not quite sure how to explain what was going on. "I've talked to Andrew. Brown has been arrested, but they are confident he wasn't the one responsible for her kidnapping. He was involved somehow though."

Mark's head went back to the wall and he stared at the ceiling. "So, what you're saying is that she still isn't safe? Any leads on who else?"

Tad shook his head. "No. This has just come up today."

Mark's look was angry as he stared at Tad. "Find them, Tad. She can't take much more. She needs to know it's all over and I can take her home."

Tad nodded as he stood. "We get that, Mark. We really do. Listen, if you can get her back on the bed, I'll have Suzie take a look at her back."

Chapter 18

$\mathcal{M}$ark stood and watched as Julia slept, reaching to brush her hair back from her face. He prayed that her sleep would be relaxing and free of dreams. He turned and walked to the door, standing to watch her once again, before heading down the stairs to find Tad.

"Tad?" Mark stood in the office doorway and then entered and sat near Tad's desk. "Where are we and where do we head next?"

"Andrew's on his way out. He's come up with somewhere to put you two." Tad held up his hand as Mark protested. "We still don't have the suspects, Mark. We can't leave you two just anywhere, and you know that."

Mark nodded. "I know, but I have clients I need to be working for and so does

Julia. We need to have this over yesterday so she can start to heal."

"We're working on that, Mark." Andrew spoke as he entered the room. "We're working on it. We've identified a new suspect and Bill is working on tracking him down as well as his cohorts and friends. It takes time to do that and to build a case that will stick."

Mark nodded, anger simmering just below the surface. Then, he sighed. I know, Lord, vengeance is yours. Let me leave it there.

"So where do we go from here? I'm assuming we can't stay with Tad and Suzie for long."

Andrew shook his head. "No, that's not possible. I'm sending you to Riverville. The police chief there has a safe house he'll put you in for the next couple of days, at least until we can come up with a new plan. He'll put officers with you for protection. They won't have been seen with you, so you should be safe."

"That's what everyone keeps saying, and it's not working very well, now is it?"

Mark rose and paced. "Maybe we should just disappear on our own."

"Don't try that, Mark. It never works." Tad and Andrew both watched as he paced.

Mark turned his head as he heard quiet footsteps, then a soft voice call his name. He rose from where he had re-seated himself and went looking for Julia. She stood at the bottom of the steps, the fear on her face fading as she saw him coming towards her.

"Mark, I want to go home. No more hiding. No more running. I can't do it any more. Just take me home, please!" She knew she was begging, but she just couldn't do it any more. She just had to be home. "I need to be at my own home."

Mark pulled her to him, a kiss dropping on her forehead. "Then, that's what we'll do, sweetheart. We'll take you home." He turned as he heard Andrew and Tad behind him. "Take us home, Andrew. You heard the lady. We're not running any more. Let them come at us. We're as good as dead now, running and hiding."

Andrew was angry but knew Mark was likely right. "I can't promise to keep you safe if you do go home." He looked around Mark at Julia. "Are you absolutely sure, Julia? We need to talk about what's been going on before we go anywhere. I need to find out who in your past wants you out of the way, wants to hurt your family in this way."

Julia stared at him. "I don't know, Andrew. I just don't know."

"Someone does, Julia. Someone wants to hurt Jason in a way he'll never recover from. How do you think he'll feel, knowing you disappeared after being sold to the highest bidder? Do you even get what that means?"

Julia stared at him. "Yes, I do. I know exactly what it means. It's come back to me, what those men were saying when I was being beaten. It's not something I will ever, ever forget. I know where they were planning on sending me. Do you think I don't know there's a million dollar pay out in a bank account somewhere that has my name on it? You're not getting it, though, are you? You think Brown was the one. He wasn't." She was in tears at this point. "He never was. He laundered money for them,

194

for their criminal activities, but he wasn't the mastermind.   That person is still out there, hidden in the woodwork somewhere. Keeping me hidden is just putting other women and girls at risk. Can you live with that?"

The three men stared at her, almost shocked at her words.

"They said that in front of you?" Andrew came closer, his eyes on her face, intent on what she had said.

She nodded. "They did. They didn't care if I heard or not." She turned back to Mark.   "There's a woman in there somewhere. I know the voice but I couldn't put a name to her." She looked up at Mark. "Take me home, Mark. Please? I can't do this anymore."

Mark reached and pulled her to him, his arms holding her tight as she wound her arms around him. "Then, that's what we'll do, Julia. We'll take you home."

Andrew was shaking his head. "Not a good idea, Mark.   We still have to find them."

Mark looked up, eyes narrowed, with a hard look on his face. "And you'll never find them if she stays hidden, now will you? She can't live the rest of her life like this, and frankly, neither can I. So you either make arrangements to take us home and bring Jason and Maria back, or we go on our own."

Tad and Andrew shared a look, Andrew finally nodding. "All right then. We'll take you home. But we need to get some security set up for you first."

Mark nodded, then arm around Julia led her to the living room. "It's today, Andrew. It has to be today."

Tad watched them walk away from him and turned to Andrew. "He's right, you know. They can't live like this for the rest of their lives. This may be the step to catch whoever it is."

Andrew nodded as he stepped to where he could see Mark and Julia. "I think it will be. She's putting herself out there, you know, to try and end this. I don't like it, Tad. I'll need to put people in place."

"Andrew, call in one of the security teams we work with. Don's available for the next week to ten days. He called me this morning, offering his team if we needed them."

Andrew turned. "Don? I never thought of him. Can you call him for me and have him meet me at Julia's place so we can go over security? Jason left me keys and the security code."

Tad nodded as he walked to the door with Andrew. "I'll do that. His is a good team, small but mighty, as they say."

Andrew stood by his car, staring around. Okay, Lord, who is it that we're after? We have suspects but no real proof. That's what we need, Lord. Lead us to that.

Chapter 19

$\mathcal{A}$ week later, Mark turned as Julia approached, a file folder in her hand, a frown on her face. She stopped in front of him, reading the pages inside.

"Mark, do you remember seeing a man named Reggie around here?"

He shook his head as she looked up at him. "No. I don't remember anyone by that name. Why?"

"Because I have paperwork here that says he was a client for four months. That's not right." She looked up at him, eyes narrowed as she thought. "Someone's playing games with my billing and my clients." She spun on her heels heading back for her office, Mark following.

"Let me see your program, Julia. I have a friend who can figure it out too. You should know him."

"Who?"

"Noah."

She stopped abruptly. "That's right. Noah. He can take a look to see where the program was hacked and when." She spun to face him. "Call him. See what he can do."

"I can't guarantee he's free."

"If the Lord wants him to look at it he'll be able to." She sighed. "There's something going on here, Mark. I have no idea what this means."

"What it means it that someone has likely hacked your program." Mark reached for the folder. "May I?"

"Please. I don't need anything else. I have enough to deal with."

Mark studied her face and noted the worry lines that had deepened even more since she had returned home. "Are you sleeping at all, Julia?"

She didn't look at him. Then she sighed. "Not really. If I get an hour or two at a time, I'm lucky. Nothing is working, Mark. I want this over. I'm tired of looking over my shoulder."

"I know you are, sweetheart. Look, why don't I talk to whoever's on watch today and see if we can get out for a while?"

She stared at him, a look on her face he couldn't understand. "Thank you, Mark. That would be nice, but our guards would never allow it, you know." She turned, her ponytail swinging as she did so, heading back for her office.

Mark sighed, watching her, knowing she was covering up a world of hurt that she was burying deep inside. *Lord, she's fighting a battle no one else can fight for her, except You. Heal my lady, please, Lord.* He turned as well and went to find Don, to see if there was really any chance of them getting out for a bit.

Don listened as Mark brought up his plan, his eyes narrowed. "Let me see what I can do, Mark. It might not be today, but we'll get you and your lady out for a bit." Don knew just how dangerous it would be for those two and how difficult it would be for him to arrange, and he already knew Andrew wouldn't like it, not one bit. Don also knew his team would be heading out the next day for another assignment, leaving these two on their own.

❁ ❁ ❁ ❁

Mark watched as Julia wandered along the town street, stopping to greet friends and acquaintances. His eyes lifted to study the area around. Then, he sighed. He had no idea who he would be looking for, now would he? Don had arranged for them to head into town, an off-duty officer with them. Don's team had had to head off. Mark was grateful for the time they had been with him and Julia but now they were on their own. Would they survive?

Julia turned to find Mark beside her, reaching for her hand.

"Mark?" Her voice was hesitant.

"It's okay, Julia. I just don't want to lose you anywhere along here. What was it you were really looking for?"

"Maria has a birthday coming up and I'm need to find a gift. I'm not usually looking at almost the last minute." Momentary panic flickered across her face. Then she stopped as she heard a voice. Her hand tightened on Mark's.

"Julia?" Mark looked around, not sure what had just happened. "Julia?"

She shook her head. "Nothing. I just thought I heard the woman's voice. But that's not possible, is it?"

Mark shrugged, then pulled her along the sidewalk with him. "Let's get your gift for Maria, and then head home. Noah said he'll have something for us today."

Mark pulled out his phone as it chimed. "Noah? Hi. We're good. What do you find? I see. That does explain a lot, doesn't it? No, we're downtown right now, but I can call you later. I see. Give us a couple of hours and we should be back at Julia's. Thanks, Noah." He thoughtfully pocketed his phone, eyes staring into the distance without seeing the historical buildings of the town, the throngs of townspeople and tourists or the sunlight glinting off the windows. A soft word from Julia caught his attention.

"Mark? What did Noah find?"

"He found something, but I need to access your computer for him. He'll call us back. Let's get what you need and then head home."

"Home? Since when did it become your home?" Julia looked surprised at his words.

Mark stopped, heedless of the people moving around him, his eyes on her face, his feelings in his eyes for her to read. "Since I found you, Julia. Since I found you."

Mark studied the data Noah was bringing up for him. "They went that deep, did they, Noah? Wow! They're really after her, aren't they?"

"They are, Mark. Stay close to her. This is far from over. I have a search program running right now to track back, but it's coming from somewhere in town. I have a couple of names for you to pass on to Bill."

Julia turned as she heard steps behind her and both Jason and Bill approached, faces stern. She sighed. There goes my freedom again, doesn't it, Lord? I just can't run and hide any more.

The two men waited and watched as Mark finished off his work with Noah, then turned in his chair, handing a slip of paper to Bill.

"Noah came up with these two names. I'm sure you'll recognize them both. He's tracked the hacking to somewhere here in town."

Bill took the paper, reading the names, his face grimmer than ever. "Thanks, Mark. They're two we've been looking at." He looked between Julia and Mark. "I need to talk to you two, and I already know you're going to fight me on what I have to say."

"Then, let's say you said it, we've fought you, and moved on?" Mark tried to inject some humour into the situation.

"Funny, Mark." Jason gave a quick grin before his eyes went to his sister. "Julia, Brown was run down and killed this morning."

Julia's hand went to her mouth and she leaned back on Mark as he wrapped his arms around her. "No! Who?"

"We have a description of the vehicle, but it more than likely will be stolen." Bill watched the conflicting emotions crossing her face. "They've taken out someone who can identify them, Julia. Chances are they'll come looking for you."

"I'm through running, Bill. Let them come. I want this over yesterday. I need it over." Tears sparkled in her eyes for a moment until she willed them away. "I want to go on with my life." Her hands wrapped around Mark's and Bill noted the ring she was now wearing.

They really had to go and do that, didn't they, Lord? Now what? They'll use Mark even more to get to her. How do we keep them away from danger?

Jason studied his sister, seeing the hardness that had come into her face and eyes. "Julia, think about it for a moment."

She shook her head, pulled away from Mark and walked across the office, turning at the doorway to study both Jason and Bill before her eyes raised to Mark, who nodded. They had talked about what they wanted to do, and the time had come. They had no security on them now and they would just refuse it if it was offered.

"Julia?" Bill questioned her with his voice. "What are you two up to?"

Mark turned to share a look with Julia, then turning his head, spoke to Bill. "We're going on the offensive, Bill. No more waiting around for them to try and snatch Julia."

"Just what are you two planning?" Bill searched Mark's face.

"We've been in touch with Andrew and he's set up an interview for Julia with a local news station. She's giving an interview tomorrow morning, with scripted questions only, detailing what has happened to her."

Jason stared past Mark at his sister. "Julia?"

She turned, her eyes shadowed enough to hide her thoughts and emotions and her face wiped of any expression. "Jason? What would you have me do? Walk in fear the rest of my life? That's not happening any more. I want more than this, Jason. Much more. I feel like I've had my life on hold for too many years, have seen too many of my dreams shatter to pieces. Dreams that no one ever knew about or cared about. Mark and I want to move on, to plan our life together, and we can't." Tears sparkled in her eyes as she brushed past Jason and headed for the outdoors.

Jason stared after her, then at Mark. "Mark?"

Mark watched Jason's face. Then without a word, he too moved past him, to head for the door, to find the woman who had become so important to him.

Jason stared after them, then turned to Bill. "What's going on, Bill?"

Bill shook his head. "You live in the same house as your sister and you're that unobservant?" At Jason's questioning look, Bill continued. "You never noticed the ring she's suddenly wearing. On her left hand. On her ring finger, to be exact."

Jason spun to look at the door, then back at Bill. "No, I didn't but then I haven't been around much in the last couple of days. Now, what, Bill? Where do we go from here?"

Bill stared at him, then moved to follow Julia and Mark. "We need to talk to them, Jason, and figure out how to salvage our investigation. They're going to totally blow it out of the water."

Chapter 20

Mark watched from the sidelines as Julia spoke with the news interviewer, her comments concise and emotionless. He prayed they had made the right move, that this would take them to the next step in finding Julia's abductors. He knew Bill had off-duty officers around, but he didn't feel that would be enough. He turned his head as he felt someone beside him. Bill stood there, shaking his head, not able to say anything as the interview concluded.

Mark moved away from Bill and found Julia, pulling her away from the set and towards the outside doors. He waited for a minute as they stood outside, then pointed at a vehicle parked nearby.

"I had Zeke drop off my car, Julia. We need to get you away for the day." He tucked her inside his car, shutting the door as he watched the emotions on her face. He slid behind the wheel and was gone before Bill or his men could find them

"Where are we heading, Mark?" Julia stared around, trying to determine just exactly where he was headed. Then, her eyes grew round as she saw the driveway he was pulling into. "Mark! We can't go in here! The owners will never let us."

Mark pulled to a stop, then turned the car off. He sat for a moment staring out the window, then shifted in his seat so he could watch her face. "You told me one day this was your dream home but that you figured you would never be able to afford it, even if it ever came on the market. Josiah's Faith is friends with the owner's daughter. She knew you would like this place. It hasn't gone on the market yet. I have first refusal on it." He got out and walked around to open her door, holding out his hand. "Come on, sweetheart. Let's walk through and see if it's really what you want."

Julia sat for a moment, then reached for Mark's hand. "Mark? We can't afford this."

Mark nodded his head. "We can. The daughter and I have worked out a deal, fair to both of us. She wants the house sold and occupied. You want this. No, you need this. You need to have some of those shattered dreams of yours come true. I would like to be the one to help those happen. You've made one of mine come true by agreeing to be my sweetheart forever." He stopped her at the door and turned her to face him, tilting her head up to look at him. "I love you, Julia, more than I ever thought I could love anyone here on earth."

She reached up a hand to touch his face, tears glimmering in her eyes. "Thank you, Mark. You're helping me to heal." She reached up to kiss him, Mark not wanting to let her go.

Walking through the house, Julia felt herself relaxing. It was a house she could make into a home very easily. She stood looking out the back door. Mark found her and wrapped her in his arms.

"What are you thinking about, sweetheart?"

"There's a building back there, Mark, that looks as if we could transform it into a clinic for me. The library would be perfect for your office." She turned to look up at him, feeling safe in his arms. "Can we do this?"

"It's already done. I just got off the phone with the daughter. We need to meet to sign the paperwork, but for all intents and purposes we have a home." He studied her face. "Are you sure?"

She nodded. "Maria loves the house that was our parents. I know it was to come to me, but I want to sign it over to them."

Mark hugged her, then walked her back through the house, locking the door behind them, before tucking her into his car. He stopped, staring around, not feeling the eyes on him that day. Where are they, Lord? Why don't I feel them? That's You, I know. You've kept them away.

"Where are we heading, Mark? This isn't the way home." Julia stared around, not quite sure what Mark was up to.

"I'm taking back our lives, Julia. Maria is meeting us in Oak City. You're going looking for a dress."

She turned, her mouth rounded, eyes big. "A dress?"

Mark nodded, a grin on his face. "A dress. You know, long, white, pearls, lace."

She smacked him as she laughed. "You're bad, you know that, don't you?"

He nodded, an unrepentant grin on his face. "Maria wants to help. Jason's not able to be with her, but I asked Faith to come along."

"I've never really gotten to know Faith, even though we went to school together. I guess I'll have to, won't I?"

"Only if you want to. But seeing as she's married to a good friend, it would probably be wise." That earned him another smack. Eyes on the mirror, he frowned, not sure if he was being followed or not, but his gut told him he was.

"Are we being followed, Mark? I can feel something."

Mark nodded. "I think we are. We'll not hiding any more, Julia. I know you're done with that."

She nodded as well. "I am, Mark. I want to get on with my life, and I can't while they're still out there."

Mark shut the door after her later that afternoon, then stood, his eyes raised to meet those of a man standing staring at him. The man walked towards him, Mark moving away from the car, locking the doors behind him, knowing Julia's eyes were fixed on him.

"Can I help you?" Mark stopped in front of the man.

The man stared past him, then looked at Mark. "That's Julia, isn't it?"

Mark nodded. "And you would be?"

The older man sighed. "I only want to talk with her for a moment. Can we go somewhere?"

Mark stared at him, then nodded at a cafe in front of them. "In there. Don't try anything though. I won't let you harm her."

"I don't mean to. I just need to talk with her."

Mark watched as the man turned for the cafe, then returned to Julia, opening her door and squatting down beside her. "Do you know him, Julia? He's asked to speak with you."

A thoughtful look on her face, she nodded. "I do. That's Dominic's father. I haven't seen him since Dominic's funeral. Did he say what he wanted?"

"He wants to talk with you. I said we'd meet him in the cafe. If you don't want to, I'll go in and tell me." He watched as she studied the cafe, emotions flickering across her face.

"No. I need to do this. This will close off a chapter that has never closed. I always liked Fred. He tried to get Dominic help but it just never worked out. He never spoke to me after the funeral and I never knew what he was thinking, if he blamed me." She turned and reached for Mark's hand. "I need you there, Mark."

"I will be. I'm not leaving you. One thing I will do. Josiah, Faith and Maria have left. I'm going to send a text to him, asking me to call or text me in 30 minutes and where we are and who we're with. Just a precaution, sweetheart."

She nodded, then took his hand to rise from the car. "I hate we have to do that. How did Josiah and Faith ever get through it?"

Mark slid into the seat beside Julia and reached for her hand. He studied the man across from him, reading the stress on his face. Lord, guide our words. You've placed us here at this time.

"Julia." Fred stopped, his eyes on the young woman sitting across from him. "I never talked to you after Dominic's funeral. Your parents never let me. They blamed me, rightly or wrongly, for what happened."

"I never did, Fred. Dominic made his choices. So did I. But I will say, I would never have gotten into the car with him that night had I known he was high on both drugs and alcohol. Maybe he would still have been alive if I hadn't."

Fred shook his head. "If it hadn't been that night, Julia, it would have been so other night. He was determined that no one else would have claim you as a girlfriend or wife. The drugs and alcohol changed him so much we couldn't reason with him or even stop him." Fred placed a notebook on the tabletop. "I've been carrying that around for the last year, trying to get up my courage to come face you. Jason warned me not to when I ran into him about six months ago."

"Jason was out of line. It wasn't his decision to make." Her finger touched the book. "Tell me, what does it say?"

Fred sighed, his eyes going to the window. "Dominic had turned into someone we didn't know any more. He was so far into drugs, not just taking them but dealing them as well, his mind was clouded." He brought his eyes back to Julia. "I don't know what he had actually planned that night, Julia, but I doubt a wedding was in the works."

Julia nodded. "I've come to that conclusion too, Fred. You and Anna tried your best but he made his decisions. I'm sorry he had to die."

Fred wiped tears from his eyes. "Thank you, Julia. I should have spoken to you before this. I saw your interview this morning. You have more courage in your little finger than I do. I have had names for years I need to turn into the police and haven't, fearing repercussions. Anna and I have talked. We're tired of living in fear. We let go of our dreams, where we wanted to be, what we wanted to do. I have kept track of you, Julia, just because I wanted to make sure you were safe." He rose and stood, staring down at the two. Then he pulled out an envelope, handing it to Mark. "Pass this on, please?" He walked away before they could say anything.

"What just happened, Julia?" Mark shifted in his seat so he could watch her face.

She stared out the window, lost in thought. The chiming of Mark's phone brought her back to the cafe and Mark.

"I'm not sure, Mark, but we need to go. Someone's out there. We need to get what we've been given somewhere safe."

✪ ✪ ✪ ✪

Mark turned as Bill walked towards him later that night. Mark had been wandering in the backyard, trying to make sense of what was going on, trying to make plans to keep Julia safe, but he just didn't have the know how to do that.

"Mark? I got your message. What do you have?"

Mark pointed at the table on the deck. "Let's sit, Bill. It was just the strangest thing." Mark explained what had happened, and handed over the book and envelope. "Julia trusts him, and her trust is not given lightly these days."

Bill nodded. "It's not. It's because of what's happened and is still happening. Did you see anyone else around?"

Mark shook his head. "No. I didn't, but then I won't know who I'd been looking for, now would I?" Anger tinged his words and he sighed. "I'm sorry, Bill. This is all getting to me."

"I know it is. We're getting there, Mark. We've made some arrests in the lower level and are working our way up. There's someone at the top that instills such fear that no one wants to identify that person, if they even are able to."

"Man or woman?"

Bill stared at Mark. "We're thinking woman or a couple but we're still searching. They're hiding well."

Mark nodded as he stood. "Thanks for coming, Bill. I hope that helps." He stared out into the darkness, light only by the solar lights edging the yard and the stars and moon overhead, quickly being covered by rain clouds. "There's a storm brewing in more ways than one. Let's end this."

Bill stared as Mark walked away, entering the house. and then down at the paperwork in his hand and sighed. There would be no sleep for him that night. He was heading back to the department and he hoped at least one of the detectives was still there to help.

⊗ ⊗ ⊗ ⊗

Julia watched as Mark worked away, his concentration deep. She needed to talk to him, but didn't want to interrupt him. She turned to walk away as he lifted his head, turning to smile at her and holding out his hand.

"Julia? Come here, sweetheart." He pulled her down on his knee and wrapped his arms around her. "You're here. I was just thinking about you."

Julia wrapped her arms around his neck, something she had not done before. "I just needed to see you, Mark. I just needed to touch you."

Mark nodded. "Bad day? Memories?" When she nodded, he prayed for them both, but particularly for his sweetheart. When he finished, he raised his eyes to find her studying him.

"How do you do that, Mark? How do you pray with such confidence, knowing Someone unseen hears you?"

Mark shrugged. "I guess because He's proven Himself to me, letting me know I can trust Him."

She thought on his words, then nodded. "Listen, are you really busy? I'm finished for the day, and would like to go for a walk somewhere."

Mark tilted his head to study his work, then looked back at her. "I'm in a good spot to leave it. I've got searches running that will take a while. Where do you want to go?"

"Can we go walk by the river in town? I know. It's a cliche, but I love walking there. It's relaxing. It reminds me of the still waters in Psalms."

Mark agreed to that but before he let her up, he claimed her lips in a kiss. When he raised his head, Julia laid hers on his shoulder, content just to be held.

“Are you wanting to go now?” he
questioned. At her nod, he set her on her
feet, rose, and took her hand.

Chapter 21

*J*ason turned as he heard his name called and tried to place the man running towards him. Then his frown disappeared. Terry from the bank slid to a halt in front of him.

"Terry. Where are you off to in such a rush?"

"I'm looking for Mark and Julia. I had papers to drop off for him, but they weren't home. I left them in the mail box. He was specific that he'd be there."

Jason froze. "What time was that?"

"Fifteen minutes ago, maybe? He had called and said they would be out for a couple of hours and asked me to come now." Terry looked at Jason. "What's wrong?"

"Was his car there?"

Terry thought and then nodded. "Both vehicles were there. Has something happened?"

"I'm afraid so. Listen, Terry, head for the department. Talk to one of the detectives, tell him or her what you told me, and stay available. I don't like this at all, not one bit."

Jason's calls for both Julia and Mark went unanswered. He searched the house and the building that housed Julia's clinic. They weren't there. He stood in the backyard, staring around. Where are you, Julia, he questioned, his heart sinking as he did so. He knew what had happened. Somehow, they had been taken again. Lord, keep them safe. Bring them home.

Bill ran for his patrol vehicle as word came out that the two were missing, Andrew at his side.

"I have the crime scene team on their way, Bill. Let's move." Andrew buckled his seatbelt as Bill took off, sirens and lights going. "Does Jason have any idea?"

"No, he doesn't. As far as he knew, Mark was planning on working in the office all day. Julia has clients that finished at 1. So where are they?"

Grim looks on their face, the three men once again searched the house and grounds. Bill finally stopped at the entrance to the office and crouched down, eyes searching the marks on the floor.

"Andrew, I've found something."

"What?"

"If you look at it from this angle, the light shows drag marks. I would say Mark, just by the type of shoe."

Andrew searched the area and followed the marks to the desk chair. He rose. "Get the team in this room first. I would say Mark didn't leave on his own."

Jason stood at the doorway, listening, pulling out his phone as it chimed. "Maria. Where are you? Stay with your Mom, please. Yeah. They're gone. What's that? You saw them when? Where were they heading? Okay. Thanks hon. That helps."

The two men with him walked back towards him, eyes on his face.

"What did Maria say, Jason?" Andrew almost barked the question.

"She saw them just after 1 when she headed to her Mom's. They were planning on going for a walk along the river, then coming back here. Mark had a program running he needed to look at around 4 or 4:30, which is when he told Terry from the bank to be here." Jason spun and headed for the door.

"Jason, hold on. You're not heading there." Bill caught his arm and stopped him. "I'll send patrol officers there. We need you here."

Jason stopped, torn between two places, and finally turned. "What can I do?"

"We wait until the places are processed, then we go back through." Andrew turned, feeling like he was being watched. "Someone's out there, fellows, watching us. We'll go through the buildings, Jason, and see what we can find." He walked towards Mark's vehicle, surprised to find the door unlocked. "Does he usually lock the door?"

Jason and Bill shared a look, before Bill spoke. "Always. He's always reminding us to lock it or lose it."

Andrew nodded. "We'll need the team to go over this as well."

Andrew turned as Bill approached him two days later, a folder in his hand, a frown on his face.

"Did they find anything, Bill?"

"Nothing. Not in the house, the outbuildings, Mark or Julia's cars. Not a thing."

"Nothing? That doesn't surprise me, but why?" Andrew paced towards his office, Bill in step with him. "How's Jason?"

"Hurting. I've put him off on stress leave, until we find them."

Andrew nodded. "A good move." He pointed at a chair near his desk and then closed the door. "Bill, you're from this town. Talk to me about it. I'm hearing rumours of a group of business owners that have organized to fight crime in your town. Josiah and Faith won't answer when I come right out and ask them, but I know someone contacted them."

Bill drew in a deep breath. "There have been rumours for years of this. Faith's father was one of the original ones as well as her uncle, I think. They never say who is

226

involved but I know at least eight are in the group. They keep themselves silent, only stepping in when they need to. Like with Josiah and Faith. I'm pretty sure someone did with them. Now, Mark and Julia? It won't surprise me."

"Vigilantes?"

Bill shook his head. "No. They don't work that way. They watch their town, look for trouble, and then find the people they need to help fight it. They don't come to us because they know we're all ready fighting it."

Andrew sat back in his chair as he pondered what Bill had said, elbows on the chair arms, steepled fingers tapping his chin. "So, like the old west, we have the good guys and the bad guys?" He quirked an eyebrow at Bill, who smiled and nodded. "Okay, I can live with that. Do you think Terry is involved?"

Bill shrugged. "I can't say for sure, but it wouldn't surprise me. His family have been involved in the financial aspects of town since it was founded, I think."

"That makes sense. I wish I knew who the others were. But they work with us, and that's all we can ask." He leaned forward, elbows on the desk. "Now, how do we find those two?"

Bill shrugged. "I'm all out of ideas. I have no clue now where to look for them."

Andrew rose at the tap of his door, surprised to see Jason there.

"Jason, come in. I thought you were off on leave?"

Jason greeting Bill, then sat. "I am, Andrew. I just wanted to know where we stood."

"Right now, Jason, I have to say we're working through what we've gathered."

Jason snorted. "There wasn't anything there. I could tell." He looked down at his hands, silent for a moment, then looked up at Andrews, tears shimmering in his eyes. "I can't lose her, Andrew. She's all the family I have left. Where is she?"

Bill's hand dropped on Jason's shoulder in compassion. "We're looking, Jason. Did Terry say what paperwork he left for Mark?"

Jason stilled, his eyes narrowing. "Mark had bought the old Reilly house and that was the final paperwork. Do you think..?" His voice dropped off.

"We'll check it out, Jason. Right now, we need you at home, just in case you get a call there. Julia's phone was left there, so they may call you on that." Andrew nodded at Bill as he hauled Jason to his feet and hand on his shoulder, directed out the door and to Bill's car.

Andrew turned from his car, looking around the old Reilly place. He had never been here before, but he decided it was a nice place to live. He didn't like the way the forest was so close. He walked towards the house, then headed around to the back, eyes to the ground, searching. He lifted his eyes, feeling someone watching him, then walked towards the outbuildings.

He searched the buildings and then turned to the house, pulling out the key Terry had given him. He opened the back door slowly and entered, hand reaching for his weapon. Something was off, he knew. Someone other than Mark and Julia had been here, but when? Reaching the stairs, he climbed, eyes watchful, noting the footprints. There were too many to have been just Mark and Julia. A noise had him raising his head before he tumbled back down the steps to lay still and silent, his weapon loose in his hand.

The man stood over Andrew's body. Anger was rising in him. How did the police know to come here? It had been a perfect spot to hide those two. Now they would need to move them. He moved past Andrew's crumpled form and headed for the back door and through the woods to the hidden cabin. Hurtling insults and orders, he ordered them to move their two captives and hide any evidence they had left.

Hours later, the officer on patrol pulled in and stopped behind Andrew's car. He got out and walked towards the house, trying the front door and then moving around to the back, entering through the open door. Reaching the bottom of the stairs, he stopped, then dropped to his knees, hand out to check Andrew's condition. Calling for help, he searched the house, returning to open the front door for the paramedics.

Bill stood and watched as the paramedics worked over Andrew, then loaded him onto a stretcher and into the ambulance.

"What did you find?" he asked the patrol officer, nodding as he listened. "All right, spread out and search the area. Find anything you can that may be related."

He turned as he heard his name called. Jason stood on the steps.

"Jason? What are you going here?"

"I heard the call about Andrew. How is he?"

Bill squinted into the dying sun, then shook his head. "He's still unconscious. It looks as if he took a tumble down the steps. I haven't seen or heard from him since before lunch."

Jason looked around, then turned back to Bill. "This is the house Mark bought. Are they here?"

Bill shook his head. "No sign that they were ever in the house, although there were lots of footprints. I have officers searching the surrounding area."

"There's a cabin back in the woods. Did you send someone there?"

Bill spun to stare at Jason. "I forgot about that. Come on. Do you remember exactly where it was?"

Jason nodded, feet pounding as he headed for the woods. "I do. It would be a perfect spot to hide them."

They stood in the doorway of the cabin, seeing the evidence of the hurried departure.

"They were here, Jason. We've missed them."

Jason nodded, sadness covering his face. "We did, Bill." He sighed. "The crime scene team will have a time going through this place."

Bill nodded, then pointed the way they had come. "I'll send an officer to have them come this way. We'll find them, Jason."

Jason stared into the distance, watching as the stars brightened in the night sky, the birds whispering softly as they settled in for the night, the frogs in chorus from the nearby creek. "Will we be in time, Bill? Will we find them before Mark is dead and Julia gone for good?" He turned, shoulders slumped in defeat as he headed back towards the house.

Bill watched as he walked away, then turned as an officer caught his attention. "What do you have there, Dan?"

"We found this outside the cabin, near where we think they had a car parked." He held out a phone.

"Do you know whose it is?"

"It's not Mark's or Julia's. I'm heading in to the lab with it, to see what they can find on it."

"Good man. Call me."

Bill walked through the hospital emergency department about an hour later, looking for the physician treating Andrew. Finding him, he had a few quiet words, then headed for the cubicle Andrew was in. He pushed aside the curtain, standing watching his friend and supervisor, before letting the curtain drop behind him. He moved on almost silent feet to stand at Andrew's bedside, watching as Andrew moved restlessly. He had not roused from when he had been found, and the physician was concerned.

After a few minutes, Bill walked away, determination in his steps. He wanted those men bad enough he could taste it.

Chapter 22

Mark stirred, his head moving on the dusty damp floor. He rolled to his side, nausea hitting full force as he did so. His hand sought his head, finding the spot that hurt the most on the back of it. He tried to open his eyes but lost the battle and slipped back into that deep black abyss of unconsciousness. Julia watched from where she was seated, unable to move to help Mark. She breathed a small sigh of relief that he was alive and tugged at the rope holding her in place. She had roused not long before Mark had.

She searched the area, looking for something, anything, that would help free her. She found nothing. Her body drooped and she slumped back on the floor. She hadn't felt them moving her from one location to another. That scared her. She knew she had been given something in the water they made her drink. She tugged at the rope again, trying to loosen it. It just wouldn't loosen at all. Tears of frustration in her eyes, she looked around, looking for anything once more that would help. Then she too slipped back into the darkness, not seeing the man who walked heavily down the stairs and stood over her, hooded eyes watchful and greedy. She was worth money to him, he thought. Finally, after all these years, he had her in his hands.

He turned to stare down at Mark. We'll send him out as well, to some country where he'll become slave labour. I'm sure I can find someone who will take him off my hands. Other than that, his death wouldn't matter to anyone.

✪ ✪ ✪ ✪

Andrew stared at Bill, eyes blurring. "Where do we stand now, Bill? Did you find them?"

Bill shook his head. "We just missed them. They must have been in the cabin when you were searching the house. They left it in a hurry. The team says they've found evidence and are working to process it as quickly as they can. There was also a cell phone found, and we've tracked it down." When he said the name, Andrew shook his head. "I didn't know if you knew him or not, but he's been pretty vocal about crime in town."

Andrew sighed, pain coursing through his head. "I just wish I had found them."

"They're getting sloppy, Andrew. It's just a matter of time now."

"Time those two may not have." He looked towards the door as it cracked open. "John?"

John and Jonah stood there, John a little shaky on his feet yet.

"Andrew. Heard you were here." John moved towards the bed, stopping at the foot, grasping the footboard to keep himself steady. "How's the head? About that bad, is it? Listen. Jonah's told me what's happening. He also says he's heard from Noah. Apparently, Mark's program automatically fed to Noah if he didn't access it within thirty minutes of the search finishing. He's sending me the information. Mark's good. He's found who the leader is and where they're heading. My contacts are watching the plane and there hasn't been any activity there as yet."

"Where are they, John?" Bill spoke up, sharing a look with Jonah.

John swayed and with a hand on his arm, Jonah shoved his uncle down into a chair. "He's not to be up yet, but he insisted, Andrew."

Andrew started to nod, then stopped. "I know that feeling. I want out of here too but can't. So, where are you going with this information, Bill?"

Bill shot him a look even as Jonah handed him a paper with names written on it. His eyebrows rose as he read the names, then handing it to Andrew.

"Do you know these people, Bill?" Andrew watched closely as Bill struggled to compose himself.

"I do. And I would never have suspected most of them, especially the leader."

"Mark's life is worth nothing now, you know." Andrew reached for the control and raised the head of the bed more, a frown in place. "We need to find them yesterday, Bill."

Jonah spoke up, sharing a look with his uncle. "John's been trying to come up with places he's been at that, where they could hide them. Turn the paper over, Bill. We've listed a number of them, starring the ones more likely."

Bill's hand froze as he read the addresses, his eyes closing as he realized the ramifications of what John had come up with. His eyes opening, he turned to John. "You're sure on these?"

John nodded. "About as sure as anything in this life. I've been to most of them with the group. I've also heard them talk of those addresses."

"What I don't get, John, was how you managed to be in and around this town and not be recognized?"

John gave a low laugh. "That's because I left here at age sixteen, moving with my parents miles away. We never really came back here once Dad's parents were gone."

Andrew nodded, then looked at Bill. "It's your investigation, Bill. Do what you need to and pull in who you need. Contact Tad. Some of those addresses are in his jurisdiction, and Suzie may be able to help with search and rescue. Just keep me updated." He laid his head back, his face white with pain.

Jonah and Bill walked from the room, leaving John to keep Andrew company. Bill once more looked down at the paper.

"How did he know to search for this, Jonah?"

Jonah shook his head. "I have no idea. He sets up his program to search and just keeps widening the parameters of what and who he's looking for. He's good. Noah's working on something as well. Now, what can I do?"

"Find the guys and start up the prayer chain. That's the only way we'll find them before Julia disappears." Bill stopped, a look crossing his face that Jonah had never seen before. "I just pray they haven't moved her by vehicle to another airpot and taken off with her."

Jonah nodded, pulling out his car keys. "I'll get the guys working on that. Faith said she has her church's group praying round the clock."

"That will help. If John says anything more, let me know. I'm glad he's up and around."

"Me too, Bill. I'll catch up with you later."

Bill watched as Jonah walked away, then turning himself heading for his car and then the department, looking for his team and handing out assignments. Lord, let us find them, please. We need to bring them home before they are hurt any more than they already have been.

⊙ ⊙ ⊙ ⊙

Mark roused once more, feeling hands on his face. His vision still blurring, he rolled onto to his back, reaching for his head once more. A hand caught his and held it. Squinting, he tried to focus on the face hovering over him.

"Mark?" Julia's voice was quiet as she held his hand tight, her other hand resting on his chest. "Mark? Can you hear me?"

Mark nodded, pain shooting through his face. "I can. Where are we?" He had difficulty forming his words.

241

"In a basement somewhere, I think. We were moved from the cabin." Julia's eyes shot around the basement, looking for a way out. "There's no way out. I've searched."

Mark moved to sit up, his head pounding. "Help me sit up." He leaned against her as she wrapped her arms around him. "Are you okay?"

She was silent, and he turned to look at her. Mark watched the emotions crossing her face and sighed. No, she's not, is she, Lord? Any progress we've made is gone, isn't it?

"Julia? Look at me, sweetheart." He waited until her eyes finally found his, shadows in their depth. "Did they hurt you?"

She shook her head. "No. Just put something into my water that drugged me. They've hurt you, though, Mark. They've hurt you!" Tears sparkled in her eyes and tracked down her cheeks, leaving muddy tracks. "How do we get away, Mark?"

He sighed, knowing that without help, they likely wouldn't be able to escape.

"Have they said anything at all that you've heard?"

She was silent, her eyes on him. Then she gave a brief nod. "I'm still to leave the country. You, they're still debating about. One wants to kill you. One wants to send you overseas for slave labour."

Mark's arms tightened around her. "That's not happening. Andrew and Bill will find us." Mark rose, swayed for a minute until he found his balance, and then searched the room. "Here. Did you see this, Julia?"

"See what?" She didn't rise, just watched.

Mark held out his had. "Come here, sweetheart. I don't want to talk really loud." When she didn't rise, he returned to her, caught her hand, and pulled her to her feet and over to where he had been searching. He pointed at a stream of light coming through the wall. "It looks as if it's an outside entrance that isn't been closed in. We'll wait until dark and then I'll see if I can get us out." He shot a look at the stairs. "How often do they come down?"

She shrugged. "I have no idea. They've pretty much kept me drugged, just like they did before. Although today they haven't." A puzzled look crossed her face.

Mark's heart felt like it sank to his feet. No drugs today? Then they must be planning on moving them out tonight or tomorrow at the latest. He didn't have any time to waste then, did he? He turned from Julia, searching for anything that would help him dig through the door.

Finding nothing, he returned to the doors and leant on them, finding them moving towards the outdoors. "Julia, your hands are slimmer than mine. If I can get enough of an opening, can you reach through to the latch and push it up?"

Mark kept pushing at the door and finally had enough space that Julia's fingers slipped through and the latch was moved. He put a finger to his mouth and waited, eyes on the stairs. He hadn't heard any movement from upstairs.

His mouth close to Julia's ear, he asked, "Have you heard anything upstairs?"

She shook her heard. "No, I haven't. Does that mean they're not there?"

Mark hesitated, then spoke. "It might be. Come on. We need to leave. Let me go through first."

Mark slipped out the partially opened door, hoping the faint squeak of rusty hinges hadn't roused anyone's attention. He reached for Julia's hand, pulling her out with him, and then dropping the door quietly behind him. His eyes searching, he didn't see anyone. He pointed towards the garage, set off from the house. They crept towards it, eyes and ears alert. There were no vehicles in it and he couldn't see any vehicles around the house. That meant, did it Lord, that they could get away?

He grasped Julia's hand in his, fingers entwined, and ran with her towards the corn fields behind the house, pulling her into a row and along it, the corn tall enough to hide them. He finally stopped, staring behind him, eyes watchful, ears listening. He breathed a sigh of relief. So far, so good.

Julia's breath came in quick gasps. "Did we get away, Mark?"

He shrugged, not quite sure. "We need to keep moving. Do you know where we are?"

She shook her head. "I have no idea. I'm not even sure if we're still in my home area. They could have moved us miles away."

A loud noise behind them made them both jump. Then Mark grabbed for Julia and pulled her with him.

"We can't stay here, Julia. We need somewhere to hole up until we can figure out where we are and how we can get help."

She nodded. "Mark, what happens if we can't figure out where we are or can't find help?"

"Then we just keep moving."

⊙ ⊙ ⊙ ⊙

Bill stood and watched as the officers worked their way through the house, turning as one approached him.

"There was someone tied up downstairs, Bill. It looks as if whoever it was got the outside basement entry open and got away."

Bill nodded, walking around to the back of the house, then turning to look. He pointed at the corn field. "That's where they went. We'll need a canine officer out here.

"Sorry, sir. They're all tied up in the search for those missing children. But Tad's wife is an auxiliary officer."

"Good. Call her in. I have a feeling we're not that far behind them." He turned as he heard commotion from the road and headed that way, stopping to watch as vehicle doors were opened and men pulled out and handcuffed. "What's going on?"

"These are some of the suspect vehicles and suspects we were looking for, sir." The young female patrol officer approached him. "The Lieutenant had put out word yesterday to watch for them." She turned and pointed at one vehicle. "Although I am surprised to see Jim Weston there. He's pretty prominent in town."

"Jim Weston?" Bill pulled out the paper with Jonah's notes on it. "No, he's involved. He's one of the top men in it. I would hazard there's only one higher than he is. Good work. Make sure everything is done by the book. We don't want any issues."

"Yes sir." She walked away as Bill saw Tad and Suzie heading his way, her dog pacing by her side, ready to work.

"Tad. Suzie. Thanks for coming." Bill explained that he had found. "I think they made their way into the corn field, but from there I have no idea."

Suzie smiled. "We'll find them, Bill." She headed off towards the back of the house, two officers keeping pace with her.

Tad turned to watch as the patrol vehicles pulled away. "What happened?"

"They walked right into us. No warning at all." He handed Tad the paper he still held. "Here's a list of names. Recognize anyone?"

Tad studied it, then lifted his eyes. "Weston? The one who supports the police so much?" He shook his head. "Now we know why, don't we?" He handed the paper back to Bill. "That we can't use as evidence not likely."

Bill shook his head. "We can. Mark's run it as a forensics accountant and he's a consultant with the forces. So it's legit." He sighed. "I just wish I could find them." His phone chimed and he pulled it out and read the text. "Now, this isn't good." He tilted it so Tad could read it.

"She's gotten away?"

Bill stared into the darkening sky. "No. I have someone following her. We just need to connect the dots and we can arrest her. That's getting close. John's given Andrew a lot more information."

"John? He's awake?"

Bill grinned. "He is and on his feet. When I left Andrew, John was with him."

"How's Andrew?"

"Angry. Miffed. Wants out of the hospital. He's fortunate, Tad. He could easily have broken his neck. A concussion, bumps, bruises, sprained wrist and elbow. He could very easily have died yesterday."

"That he could. Look, I'm heading out to find Suzie and see where she's at. Let me know if I can help in any other way."

Bill watched Tad walk away and then turned back to the house. Lord, where are they? It's coming up to night and it looks as if rain is setting to move in. Keep them safe.

Chapter 23

*M*ark finally stopped, dropping to the ground, and pulling Julia tight to him. Gasping for breath, he watched the direction they had come from. Out of the fields and into open fields, he had found the one tree in the centre of the field, knowing they needed to rest.

Julia's head fell on Mark's shoulder as she clung to his shirt. "Are we safe, Mark?"

"I don't know, sweetheart. I pray we are." He looked around, eyes narrowing, and then looking up at the stars, slowly being covered by the clouds moving in. "We need to find shelter somewhere. Rain's moving in."

She nodded and sat up, pushing her hair back from her face, twisting it into a knot on her neck. She stared at the scratches and bruises on her hands, then like Mark, stared around her. "I think I know where we

250

are now, Mark. There should be a cave up ahead we can shelter in overnight. If I remember, it's pretty sheltered."

Mark finally stood, his hand reaching for Julia. "Okay. Which way?"

Julia pointed. "That way. Mark, I hope we make it. I don't like the feeling I'm getting."

He nodded, his face barely visible in the dark. "Can you see all right in the dark?"

She gave a snort. "Not really but we don't have a choice, now do we?"

Mark stopped her. "First, let's pray, okay?"

She shrugged. "Whatever."

Mark's heart sank at her words. Where did her faith go, Lord? Has what she's been through enough to totally destroy that?

✪ ✪ ✪ ✪

Suzie turned as Tad caught up with her. "I'm still following them, Tad, but we need to take a break."

251

Tad nodded, then pointed to a clear area. "There. That should do it." He pulled out a bottle of water and a collapsible dish from her backpack and give the Border collie a drink. "How far ahead are they?"

"The scent's still fresh, so not that far ahead. The rain's moving in. If we don't find them soon, I don't know if we will."

Tad nodded, then repacking the backpack, pulled her to her feet. "Let's keep moving then, as quickly as we can." He pulled out his flashlight, the beam large and wide. "This will help, I think. I've put in a call for more search and rescue personnel, but they're still tied up on that other search."

Suzie nodded, then watched as her dog alerted. "They're around here somewhere, Tad. Watch." She was almost into a run as her dog pulled her forward. She slid to a halt as the dog headed for an opening the hill, stopping to give a low bark.

Tad motioned Suzie to wait and moved forward.

"Mark? Julia? It's Tad. Are you there?"

Mark appeared at the entrance of the cave, Julia tucked behind him. Relief coloured his face.

"Tad! Suzie! How?"

"Bill found the house you were held in and called Suzie in. She's been following you for a while. Are you two okay?"

Mark and Julia shared a look. "About as well as we can be." He stared at Tad. "There's more, isn't there?"

Tad nodded. "Look, come on out here. We have some food and water for you. Sit. Eat. We'll talk as we do."

Julia sank down, grateful for the blanket Suzie wrapped around her. "Is it over?"

Tad shook his head. "Not quite. We still have to arrest the one in charge, but we have everyone under her."

"Her?" Mark's jaws stopped moving, then he chewed on his sandwich again. "A woman?"

Tad nodded. "Julia was right when she said she heard a female voice." He pulled out his phone and looked at the text message. "Good. We have transportation on the way. We'll get you to the hospital and get you checked out."

Julia spoke up. "Why did they move us from the cabin?"

Tad and Suzie shared a look. Tad looked down before he spoke. "Andrew found the house and was hurt. They moved you because they knew we'd find the cabin. Jason remembered it. They were a little careless. One of them lost their phone."

"Is Andrew okay?" Julia searched Tad's face.

"He's a bit battered, but he'll survive. He'll be glad to hear we found you two." He looked past them as he heard vehicles. "Sounds like our transportation's here. Let's get you home."

❂ ❂ ❂ ❂

Bill turned as Tad walked towards him, his footsteps on the tile flooring echoing through the hospital corridor.

"Tad?"

"We have them, Bill. They're downstairs in Emerge, being assessed. Suzie and her dog came through again."

254

Bill's eye slid shut in relief. "What about the leader?"

"I was going to ask you about her. Any signs of her around town?"

Bill shook his head. "It's like she's just packed up and left but I know she hasn't. I have a friend running a search for properties she might own. I don't think we're quite over this yet."

"Andrew awake?" Tad pointed at the room door.

"He wasn't but we can wake him. John's been with him all day and is still there." Bill cracked the door open, then entered.

Jason stood at his sister's bedside, watching as she slept. Please, Lord, heal her heart as well as her body. She'll never be the same but bring her back to me. Maria slid her arm around him and hugged him, tears sparkling on her cheek.

Mark stood in the doorway, watching the siblings, then turned, heading for the chapel. His family wasn't here, and he could really handle having them messing in his life again. His parents he knew were overseas, on a short-term mission, his brothers, one in school, one at his own church. He would call them later. He needed to take Julia to meet them. He sat, his eyes on the cross at the front, his thoughts on the past few weeks, then centring on the woman sleeping on another floor. He prayed for her healing. He ignored the sound of the opening door, his mind and thoughts focused on his God.

When he stood, he stopped, staring at the woman in front of him, a puzzled frown on his face.

"Do I know you?"

The woman shook her head. "No, you don't, but you will. You're coming with me." A weapon appeared in her hand. "Now move."

Mark's hands went up in the air. Who is this, he wondered? "What do you want with me?"

"You cost me millions, buster. You're going to pay and then that thing downstairs will pay as well. So will anyone who gets in my way."

Mark stood still, his mind racing. This was the mastermind, the one behind it all? He wouldn't have thought that at all.

"Where are we going?"

"Out of here." She waved her weapon at the door. "Now move, unless you want to die right here."

Mark shook his head, passing her, watching as the weapon remained steady on him. He left the chapel, heading for the stairs as she directed.

"We need a passcode to get out, you know." Mark's voice was conversational in tone.

"I have that." She punched in the code, then shoved him through. "Down the stairs."

Mark sighed, knowing he wouldn't be able to overpower her on the stairs. Once outside the hospital, she again shoved him forward, towards the back of the parking lot. Sudden lights temporarily blinded them and Mark took advantage of that fact to run. A sudden crack and Mark was falling, darkness following him.

Tad was headed in the building and stopped as he heard the shot. Pulling his own weapon, he ran for the sound, watching as the woman approached the form on the ground. He could hear security calling and footsteps behind him.

"Stop! Police!" Given no choice when the woman refused to stop, Tad pulled the trigger and watched as she fell. He ran towards her, kicking the gun away, and felt for a pulse. Judgement had come. She would face a higher Judge than an earthly one, he thought. He turned his attention to the form on the ground, crouching to feel for a pulse. His heart fell as he realized it was Mark. How?

Bill looked around as Tad appeared in the doorway, hesitating before entering. He saw the sadness on Tad's face.

"Tad?"

"We got her, Bill. I had to shoot her." He stopped speaking, his eyes going past Bill to Andrew. "She shot Mark, Andrew. Somehow, she got to him and shot him. They're working on him now."

"How bad?" Andrew asked the question none wanted to ask.

"His back. They'll be taking him to surgery soon, but they're not sure how much damage has been done." Tad turned to the door. "I need to go find Julia."

"Tad, wait." Bill approached. "Are you sure you need to tell her tonight?"

Tad nodded, his eyes fixed ahead of him. "I do. It's not something that she'd forgive us for it we didn't."

Chapter 24

Julia turned from the window in Mark's hospital room a week later, her eyes seeking the face of the man she loved. *Why, Lord? Why did You let him get hurt? It wasn't necessary at all. I just don't get it.*

Mark roused from his sleep, eyes not quite focusing. He turned his head as Julia stepped to the bed, hands gripping the side rail.

"Julia?"

"Mark. How are you feeling?"

He shook his head. "Not great. The pain's bad today. Is that a good thing or a bad thing?"

"A good thing, I think. If you weren't feeling pain, they would be worried. You're almost due for another shot of pain medication." She reached for the call button, but his hand stopped him.

"No, Julia. It clouds my mind too much." He studied her face. "You're hurting too. Talk to me."

She stared in the distance, biting her lip, before bringing her gaze back to him. "Why, Mark?"

"Why what?"

"Why did God let you get shot, when we were safe?"

Mark shrugged. "I have no idea, sweetheart. God's ultimately in control."

"That's what I'm talking about." She poked his shoulder a little harder than she meant to. "Why did He let any of this happen?"

"I don't know. I don't have that answer. But I do know that I need to trust Him fully, that I need to rest in the confidence that He really does have a plan and purpose for whatever I go through."

"How? How do you have that confidence?" Tears laced her voice as they streaked her face. "I don't have that, not any more, Mark."

He reached for the side rail, putting it down, then tugged her down and into his arms, grimacing as he did so, but ignoring the pull and pain. "Then we pray you get it back. You've changed, Julia. You'll never be the same again. None of us will. We need to move on. God provides us healing, we just need to reach out. It's not instantaneous. It comes over time. If we need to seek counselling, we'll do that."

She sighed, knowing in her head what he said. "I just hurt so much, Mark. I almost lost you. You'll have a long recovery ahead of you."

Mark tightened his arms as he prayed for the words he needed. "We'll get there, sweetheart. Doesn't matter how long. Just keep that hand of yours in His. He has a strong grip and will hold on to you." He stopped, eyes closing against the pain he was in. "Just trust, sweetheart. Ask Him to help you trust. Those dreams you think are shattered? God will take them and make something even more beautiful out of them."

She nodded, her eyes thoughtful. "I've doubted, questioned, blamed. All over the last few months. Actually it likely goes back to Dominic."

"It likely does but that chapter is now closed and in the past. We have a brand new chapter of our own to write."

She leaned back to look at him. "We do, don't we?" She reached to kiss him, then snuggled back on his shoulder. "Where now, Mark?"

"We claim back our lives. We claim back our house we're making into a home. We claim back who we are." He sighed. "It's going to be a struggle but God's promised not to leave us alone."

Bill hesitated before entering as he heard the two talking, but he really needed to talk to them.

"Mark. Julia." He approached the bed, watching the two in front on him. "How are you, Mark?"

"Getting there. Thankful there was no real damage done. How'd that happen?"

"By what the surgeon said, you were moving away from her and going towards the ground when she fired." Bill stopped, at a loss for words. "I'm sorry, Mark, Julia. I should have known."

Julia shook her head. "She hid her activities well, Bill. Gwen Strong was an accountant for years, well respected in the community. Who would have thought of her being involved in money laundering, drugs, human trafficking? She just didn't seem the type."

"I know, but she almost cost you both your lives. How do we live with that, you two?"

"Ask for forgiveness, put your trust back in the Lord, and move forward." Mark knew it would be difficult.

"You sure you're not a preacher, Mark?" Bill asked, half in jest.

"Not a preacher but the son and brother of one."

Bill nodded, then raised his eyes to the window, watching the reds, golds and purples of the sunset, praying for healing for all involved.

"Listen, I'm heading out. Zeke has some wild plan he wants me involved with."

Mark started to laugh, then stopped at the pain. "It's likely some storm he wants you to go watch with him. Go. Have a great time. Remember that in the midst of any storm, God is there. We have evil all around us but He is much stronger that than. You've managed to round up everyone involved and are working through the paperwork and charges. Go, take a break, Bill."

Bill nodded and walked to the door, turning to study the couple behind him. Thank you, Lord, for restoration.

Epilogue

Three months later, Mark turned to watch as Julia walked towards him, the long white gown in place that he had taken her to buy. It had been a struggle, he thought, overwhelmed by her beauty. He reached for her hand, grasping it tight in his, feeling the tremors shaking it.

Later, he stood, arm around her as they watched their friends and family wander the backyard of their home, content to have the woman he loved in his arms. They would be leaving shortly for two weeks just by themselves but for now they would share their time with the others.

Julia moved slightly, watching her brother and his wife.

"What are you thinking, sweetheart?" She tilted her head back so she could watch him.

"I'm just so thankful to be here, Mark, here with you and all of these people. It was too close."

"Way too close. I never thought when I had that accident that I would meet you. And that accident is what started it all off. Someone trying to stop the investigation of that leading to your abduction and then the arrests in all those crimes." He hugged her tighter.

"It was, Mark." She stopped. "Bill and Andrew were by the other day. Most of the people had made plea bargains, but we'll have some trials to go through." She paused again. "What I don't understand, and I know we've talked this over, is how you never lost your faith, your trust, when I did."

"You didn't really. It was there all the time. You were clinging to it, through your fear, your hurt, and even your anger. God never minds us asking why or how come or even to take whatever we're going through away. But He has a deeper purpose in place. Just remember that He knew what you would go through before you were even born. He prepared you for that. Someone else may not have come through as victorious as you did."

She thought about what he said and then nodded. "You're so right, Mark. Keep reminding me of that, will you? Maybe we need to have Faith do up a stained glass something or other we can hang in the window over the front door to remind us as we leave and return that we are in the hollow of His hand."

"That we are, sweetheart." He watched as the groups shifted and changed, laughter ringing through the yard. "We are blessed in so many ways. Let's find a way to make our home a true blessing to others." He kissed her, then watched as she blushed. "Don't ever stop blushing for me, sweetheart."

She hugged his arms tighter to him. "Don't ever change, Mark. I like the preacher I have of my very own, even though he claims to be an accountant."

Dear Readers:

Shattered dreams—how many dreams have you had shatter all around you? Plans, hopes, dreams? We all have that happen to us. I have had that so many times. But what do you do with those shattered pieces? Pick them up and try to put them back together again, with all the holes in them, or give the shattered pieces to God and let Him make something new out of them?

He is with you no matter what you are going through or struggling with. I must admit, the storyline was not planned in this book. They never are in my books. Even Mark's name changed from Darius to Simeon to Mark to get the name that suited the story. Julia went through some really rough times. Yes, human trafficking is alive and well in our society. You read of it every day in the newspaper, somewhere in a town near you in North America. I can't even imagine how prevalent it is in other countries. Murders and assaults are out there as well. But just remember, the Creator, the Judge, the loving God we serve is there with each one of you no matter what you are going through.

God bless each one of you as you pick up the pieces of whatever was shattered and give them back to God, to let Him make something new and wonderful out of your lives. Look for those blessings each and every day He sends your way, to help you heal and move forward.

Ronna